And then it became a part of me,
so I would have missed it if it had gone.
I am talking about sadness.

Jean Rhys • *Smile Please*

THE AFTERWORD

The Afterword

ROMA TEARNE

GREEN BOTTLE PRESS

First published in 2025

ISBN 978-1-910804-28-5

PRINTED IN GREAT BRITAIN
BY CLAYS LIMITED, BUNGAY, SUFFOLK

For
Mollie

1994

Why don't you just leave? Catch the eleven o'clock
train, go back to where you belong and get the hell
out of my life. Finally.
I will.
Go on then. What are you waiting for? I will give
you a lift to the station.
I'm packing my bag.
Good! And next time we meet will be
at your funeral.
Fine.

Silence.

Will you talk to me at last?
Only you can provide the antidote to the curse.
Ah, so you want my help, do you? Now?
Yes. I do.

2023

Here in Venice the November light is cold and
crisp and translucent.
The air is clean, the streets are empty.
Night has passed, and morning emerges through
a gauze of cloud.

The great domes of the basilica are still shrouded
in a milky mist which wraps itself around the
bridges, turning them into vapourised ghosts.

Well, as we don't seem able to ever have
a conversation without quarrelling, I am
going to write to you instead. That way you
can't answer back.

Silence.

Today is my first day in this watery city. I
arrive on a train that runs across the bridge
over the lagoon.
The sun has not quite risen. There are fishermen
pulling up the first nets of the day, heavy with
catch, dark against the lightening sky.
A seabird skims across the water so low it seems
to swim in it. A launch speeds noisily past but
the Asian family on the other side of the carriage
is intent on what they are eating. I want to tell
them to look out of the window, but no, their
sandwiches are more absorbing.
The train begins to slow down, and we all rise
to gather our luggage, unplug laptops, switch off
phones, shrug on our coats.
Santa Lucia. Venezia.
Questo treno termina qui.
Doors hiss open letting in the scent of sea and salt
and fast-moving air.
Something cold runs across my back.

Is it you?

So, my only question is this, if you don't want to
talk, will you at least read this letter? It should
of course have been written thirty years before.
There is so much that, at the end, passed us
swiftly by; so much we never addressed. It will
do us good to have it aired finally, make us both
less restless.

I don't believe you've ever been to Venice.
What would you make of it if you could be
here with me, now.
With your eyes and mine, alighting from this
train together?
Yours skimming the surface of things, taking
in the light, complaining of the cold, staring
at the grand buildings uncomprehending, a
little sulky, resentful even, that I should have
dragged you here?
Yes, it's nice, you would say
doubtfully, when pushed.
And after that, your eternal mantra as you recall
some insignificant detail of that other place where
we once lived. And then when I complained about
these nostalgic flashbacks you would simply say,
as you have done all my life - what do you know,
you can't remember anything.
That other Eden, that demi-Paradise? That
fortress built by Nature.
Of course I remember, but not quite as you do.

It *was* a Paradise, you foolish child.
Ah! You speak. And please don't call me a
child, not at my age.
Silence, again.
Will you *ever* give up with this refugee mentality,
this migrant-without-a-home, story of yours?
Why drag up the wretched past?
Why disallow yourself a moment's delight
in this place of magic and water,
in this city of stone and Byzantine glitter?
Why *still* remain haunted by some other life?

Because - oh, I don't expect you to understand.
Look, if you are going to interrupt me, I will have
to stop writing. And to tell you frankly, I am sick
of your voice in my head. It's probably why I never
finished that last letter to you.
We left, didn't we? We left that wonderful place
we all called Paradise.
So how could it have been better?
And yes, I know I am beginning to sound
impatient, angry, sneering.

It was not our choice, you say, finally.

And then you serve me another of your famous,
frosty silences guaranteed to drive me madder
than I already am. A past master at changing the
atmosphere, your passive anger has always been
more subtle, more powerful than mine.

I am just someone who shouts, swears, hurls
abuse. Correct?

Silence.

Conversation over, we leave the train, go separate
ways ordained, joint irritation poisoning the air.
Like the ghostly bridges, you too vanish into
the rising mist.
Nightmares are made of these silences.
So now, a letter. Late in the day.
Two females, one half-grown.
Perhaps it can be no other way.
Ours is a famously tricky relationship,
and reason enough for me to put down how I feel
in words, unspoken for many years.

We have unfinished business, and I am
determined you should read this letter.
Heartsease. (God what a name!)

We both know there has never been a need to tag
the refugee, the migrant, the asylum seeker, those
people who, like us, live in the twilight zone.
At least not with electronic tags.
Rest assured all details of the other place are
forever invisibly tattooed on us.
Home cries out at every foreign port, protesting at
every border stop.
Home, carrying its baggage of sadness on its back.
Yet always, the never ending, pointless
questionnaires remain.

Place of birth?
Nationality? Broadly speaking, that is.
Asia? Africa? South America? Elsewhere?
Black, White, Other?
We are the Other.

Forgetting has never been the issue. Nor has
getting lost in the crowd.
Regrafting is what's required, though for some, I
mean you, it has not been a success story.
Too much baggage, perhaps?
Too little understanding?
Whatever the reason, we clashed.
Has your disappearance affected your hearing?
And while we are at it, why did you vanish so
abruptly? A little warning might have been polite.

I am sorry if I sound resentful but on this
beautiful morning in Venice I am trying my
best to reach you.
Sitting in the railway station drinking coffee
(the best coffee, by the way, is nearly always found
in station cafés) I continue with this letter. So
many years too late, but still, I must try to make
some sense of our fallings-out.
Outside, through thick glass windows I hear
vaporetti plough across the water, scraping the
sides of the canal as they come to a halt.
The sun is well and truly up, the mist has cleared,
the city returned to a solid state.

It is Thursday, although there is no need to tell
you this, as days of the week no longer matter to
you. I sit with my new notebook, bought from the
stationery shop next door, and stare at the people
as they come and go.
Shop workers hurrying in from Mestre.
Tourists on a pointless day trip.
Locals on their mysterious journeys to other
parts of the city.

The public address remains the same.
With places conjuring up Renaissance art.
Padua.
Verona.
Bologna.
Roma.

I came here to finish my latest novel, you
know, but after years of these unsatisfactory
conversations I am suddenly determined to write
to you, instead. To tell you what I am doing right
now, to include you in my life in ways I never have
before. I hope that having a letter in your hand
will encourage you to read it.

Why bother, given you have long stopped caring?
Besides, haven't you got rid of me finally?
No.
That is the problem.
And, I say slowly, reluctantly, I have not
stopped caring.

So, for the last time let me address those things
we should have aired long ago.
To save us from this interminable circular
wandering we are trapped in.

Silence.

OK, I know you are there.

My apartment is about 36 square metres in
total. There is little natural light. The windows
open out into a narrow passageway on one side
and a courtyard on the other. There are more
apartments in the house opposite and in one
an old man watches TV while in another live
an old woman and a cat. At night these rooms
come alive as if by magic and the beautiful
wrought-iron Christmas decorations blink among
the fairy lights.
As for me, I have a comfortable bed, a table, and a
small kitchen. I am locked away in here while all
around is the steady sound of footsteps of people
going to work, tourists dragging their suitcases.
You are my only companion during this time and
by that, I mean we speak in English.
The rest of the time I struggle with Italian.

I used to hate your way of looking back.
Stop bothering me, I used to say. Stop
bringing up the past.
It's *yours*, not mine.

Besides, I used to say that looking back is a
dangerous thing. Remember Orpheus and what
happened to him? Yet here am I doing the same
dangerous thing. Perhaps no good will come of it.
For forty years you followed me around, nagging,
complaining, criticising.
Bruising me as though I were an unripe fruit.
So often I wished you dead and one fatal day,
unthinkingly, I shared this thought with you.
Setting a curse in motion.

Perhaps that was the reason I kept returning to
Venice. I wished to get away from you and your
Paradise. I used to say, Venice, yes, that is my
special place. Forget Paradise.
Although oddly, today, I have a feeling
I am mistaken.
While you continue to repeat that all
roads lead to home.

Today as I sit here drinking my first coffee of this
trip, I am momentarily distracted by a couple at
the next table. I want to share my thoughts about
them with you. A tall man with leaves tattooed
haphazardly up his arm. Here is the list.
Magano
Acero
Frassino
Ulivo
Olmo
Quercia

Albero di biancospino
Un albero di noci
And others I can no longer name.
Is this a record of the dying trees in the world?

The other arm is tattooed with images of birds.
Scricciolo
Pellegrino
Tordo
Pettirosso
Storno
And then weirdly, one flower, *Heartsease*. The
nome-de-plume you gave yourself. I hated
it, by the way!
Just being honest.

He, the man, glances at the woman, a vague kind
of affection playing across his face.
But before long he is distracted by his phone
lighting up. Now I see real interest.
And the girl? After a greedy lunge at her brioche
she becomes sated, lifeless, eyes glazed over in
what can only be described as contentment.
They speak in English.
Her nails are dipped in blood-red varnish.
She has the look of a strange child in a fairy
tale gone wrong.
With bottle-yellow hair, taut as wire, so brittle it
might be the strings from a discordant harp.
Eyelashes curved like fat legged spiders turned
outwards from her face. She must be young, I

think. But then she stands up and I fail to envy
her youth for she has what my Italian friend calls,
'English fatness.' And close up, she looks old.

Remind me, why are you telling me all this?

It's called conversation, Heartsease. Remember?
We used to have it occasionally. A good gossip,
you used to call it.

Silence.

Time to change the subject, I see.
These days when I look at other women, I only
notice the old ones.
Ah! I see your problem. You are frightened now
that you are growing old.
Don't start. I *am* old. And besides, aren't we trying
to get on with each other?

Do you remember, when you first arrived, how
much you used to admire the English, especially
the women. And how you kept talking about their
looks? So beautiful, you used to say. Remember?
There wasn't an ugly one in sight.
There is an edge to what I am saying. I know I am
in dangerous territory.

Suddenly you say, with that matching edge in
your voice which I have always hated,
the young *are* beautiful. Only the old are ugly.
Ah, she speaks! Speak again bright angel, I laugh.

I stop writing, overtaken by rage.
God, how full of shit you still are,
Heartsease, I think.
But coward that I am I dare not say this.
You see, even now, now that we are so far apart
from each other, I remain frightened of you.
So instead, I laugh out loud hoping to cover up
my jealousy. I know how you used to admire
these English girls, the whiteness of their
skin, the symmetry of their features. How
tall they all were.

I write furiously.
Slave mentality. That's your problem.
I don't suppose you can remember how I used to
cringe every time you mentioned some girl you
saw on the bus on your way to work. On and on
you went, talking about this one's blue eyes and
that one's straight hair, while saying nothing at all
about me, your own daughter.
Hating yourself, you simply saw me as an
extension of yourself.

Idiot!
What's that you just called me?
Well, isn't it true? Did you or did you not
loathe yourself?

Fools should never become mothers.
You should learn to be more tolerant, you say.

I see you would rather have a conversation. But I
for once will do as I like. I am writing everything
down as evidence for whatever you might throw
at me in the future. It's a record of how awful
you were to me.

When I finish this letter I will get back to the
book I should be working on.
In case you are interested it is a book about a
group of women engaged in a hobby they enjoy
but are very bad at. It's meant to be a light-hearted
story. Written with no particular audience in
mind, but with the hope of making a little money.
Unlike this letter, which is written just for you
and will probably get me into more trouble.
Although, with no forwarding address I have
very little hope that it will reach you. The one
advantage is that at least no one else is going
to read it. And therefore, I have the delicious
freedom of honesty, rarely seen in life.

You and I, alone at last with no one to make
mischief between us, it's a first. I ought to
be relieved, but the truth is I am still very
angry with you.

I am not in a position to answer back.
Oh, don't give me that, you'll find a way, I know
how you operate.

By the way this isn't the first letter I have tried to
write, you know. I used to write to you, regularly,

for years. From the age of thirteen. Write them
but never send them.

Sometimes I used to draw you. Mostly I used to
turn your face into a gas mask.

It's true. The friend I showed these drawings to
would howl with laughter. She was called Cassie
by the way. Cassie understood me perfectly
because she too was angry with *her* mother. It's
a common thing, you know, this fermenting
bitterness. Like bad food it rots in the gut.

Here are some interesting facts about my friend,
Cassie, in case you are curious.

You met her, once.

She was beautiful. I mean, really lovely, not like
the girls on those buses that you saw.

Cassie's mother sent her away for the summer
while her father went into hospital for a routine
operation during which he died. Cassie wasn't
informed until after the funeral.

That's all.

Why?

Who knows.

Cassie never forgave her mother.

When she was forty, she turned one of her
dolls into a surrogate mother. She made some
small clothes out of a dress belonging to her real
mother. Then she made a coffin out of cardboard
and buried her doll-mother in the garden. It was
the older woman's punishment, to be buried
twice. I should add that Cassie sent her on her

way with a letter of explanation. Just in case
her mother could not comprehend why she
needed two funerals.

Charming! I can see why she was your friend.
Don't be shocked, these things happen. You
should be glad I am being honest.

Another thing. Although it is true I am still angry
with you, it is also true that the anger has lessened
with time. And in any case, being an extension of
you, I am also angry with myself.

Now it is late afternoon, and the winter sun falls
harshly on the waters of the lagoon.
Now I sit in a bar with its low glare
against my eyes.
Now I want a glass of wine with my lunch. I wish
to break my rule of no wine with lunch.

What d'you mean I have no will power?
Yes, I do *know* that one glass can lead to another.
So what? Stop nagging. Your voice confuses me.
Do you know how old I am?
Yes, that's correct. So, don't tell me
what to do, okay?

Since you are so interested in the young let me tell
you about the young couple at the next table. They
sit with their large glasses of Venetian wine. Two
glasses between them, untouched. I can see how
the cold creates small bubbles on the glass. Drink

up, for goodness' sake, I think. In this city of
couples, I am alone, so who will care if I have that
glass of wine, after all?
And for the purpose of this letter and the
writer you loved, I will give the couple with the
untouched wine the names of Bernard and Susan.
Wholesome English names because they look like
wholesome people. I envy their wholesomeness.

Silence.

Stopped speaking again, have you? Have you lost
interest, then? Or are you just being the passive/
aggressive Heartsease I know so well?

The couple at the next table seem breathtakingly
unaware of their environment. How is it possible
to have so little curiosity?
I can't help wondering what they are doing here.
Finally, like puppets, they come alive and begin
to talk. I bend over my plate of *chiccetti* hoping I
might hear something interesting but very soon
my hopes are dashed.
They talk of nothing at all in a colourless way,
toying with the words, bored. I can see they are
placid people.
They will never suffer heartache.
They will never get divorced.
Or lose sleep over something cruel they might
have said to each other.
They will never be cursed.
Who would want to curse people like this?

Theirs is going to be a life well lived.
Their questions are simple ones.
Where shall we put the sofa,
how good is the light in the living room,
should we buy a large house plant from the garden
centre when we get home,
are you going to trim the hedge at the back?
Nest building is what this couple with the
untouched wine are good at.

Why are you writing this rubbish? I thought you
were going to write about your terrible childhood
and the awful things I did to you, how I hurt
you? And at the same time I thought you wanted
to apologise for your part in our joint misery. I
thought you had something interesting to say but
instead you tell me about a couple who sit near
you in some café? A couple I can see perfectly
well for myself.

You old bag. Don't you understand anything?
Moan, moan, moan.
Actually, what I really want to ask is, were you
like them too, Heartsease? Once upon a time?
With a man who has no interest in anything
except his own image?
Ah! I see I scored a hit there!

Silence.

Look, I have not brought you all the way to
Venice for us to have yet another quarrel. Can

we at least try to have some sort of truce. I want
to tell you how I have been feeling all these years.
And I want to write about other things, too. I
want to share my life with you. In a way I never
have. Is that okay?

I want to ask you if the art here means *anything*
at all to you? Could I take you to look at my
favourite Bellini in the *Accademia* for instance or
shall we go to the Oriental Museum, instead?
No, perhaps on second thought that isn't a good
idea. It will only encourage you to talk of all
the stolen goods plundered from our East, you
would always say.
Will you never give up banging on about the past?
Saying this of course will cause another row.
The case of the Elgin Marbles all over again.
I don't mean to be rude but aren't you still living in
a 1930s colonial outpost? You and Leonard Woolf?
Will you never forget?
Never is such a long time.

While I have been writing, Bernard and Susan
have finished their drinks. They have now
organised their living space in London. Exhausted
by too much wine and conversation they have
fallen silent. And then Bernard has a sudden
thought that needs dealing with. He goes to the
lavatory leaving Susan free to look around. She
has that expressionless face one often sees on
under-stimulated women.

How many under-stimulated women do
you know, then?
(Ah yes, there it is again, *that* wretched
amusement in your voice. How it grates.)
I am not going to listen to you. If you want to talk
to me, then do so in writing.
As you very well know, where I am now it isn't
possible to write.

Break free, Susan. Break free while you can. If you
have a girl-child, you will fight with her. Believe
me, I know what I am talking about.
Then like a genie popping out of a bottle Bernard
returns and it is Susan's turn to go to the lavatory.
Bernard seeks comfort in his phone, smiling,
stroking it as he never strokes Susan.

You make it up as you go along, don't you? It's
almost always fiction with you.
Once again, the amusement in your voice.
Sorry to snap but have you forgotten I
am a novelist?

Right on cue Susan's back, eyes alight, plenty to
recount. She's had an adventure of sorts, she nods.
The lock on the toilet door was stuck.
I might have been locked in there for ever.
She smiles, contemplating the thought.
Bernard grunts, listening.
Sort of.

It's so good they have each other. This way they
can talk about the locks on toilet doors forever.

Do you think companionship and
therefore happiness is talking about a toilet
door, Heartsease?
Why don't you answer?
Does coupledom stop a woman from engaging
with the world around her?
Still no answer.
Are we just programmed to build nests?
As you do not answer I think that perhaps you
agree. We are just nest builders and nothing more.

Did you know that homelessness is now a
lifestyle choice.
Apparently, it's official.
The woman who first announced this news is
the child of immigrants, herself. The irony of her
words seemed lost on her.
It's lost on all of us too, in Britain. Instead of
outrage there is only silence.

Why are you so surprised? We refugees might
have been the same had power come our way.
And then you add,
A person with nothing will always set great
value on power.

Well, I agree. I too am burdened with the world's
anger. It's all rolled up together like a bale of

hay. You harvested that rage long ago and kept
it safe for me.

When I was nine you read me a poem about a
homeless woman.
All she wanted was to own a dresser on which she
could place some beautiful blue and white plates.
Was homelessness already on your mind
when I was nine?

Sometimes I envy the *way* in which you messed
up your life. There was glamour to the mess. Did
you see yourself as Audrey Hepburn, on the back
of a *motorino* in *Roman Holiday* as you threw in
your lot with love?
And although it was love in a climate of
indifference, still, it *was* love.
You shouted that word from the rooftops, turned
his photograph into a shrine.
Encircled it with fresh flowers every day.
Love in its fleeting moment of wild abandonment.

How do I know all this? Don't you
remember telling me?

These days love's face is more sordid, more of an
obvious exchange; worldly goods and emotions
changing hands with ease. So no, I know no one
quite as stylish as you were.
Then.

When I tell this to your granddaughter and
her friends you should see their amused faces.
Marriage? they ask. That's for old people.
Their lives are messed up in other, more
realistic, more prosaic ways. Bypassing all those
untamed emotions.
And learning of this I realise how proud I am
of your daring sophistication, your wanton
abandonment. If only you had put your sense of
style to better use and been more like Chanel,
or Edith Piaf, or, more recently, Vivienne
Westwood. Do you even know who I mean?
No.
You might have designed clothes.
Or become an actress.
Or a well-known writer.
You were clever enough for all these things. But
feminism was occurring elsewhere and by the
time it circumnavigated the globe, arriving at your
door, you had fled the nest on your winged feet.
Black Eros would let you down long before you
encountered him in Piccadilly Circus.
What a waste.

My inheritance from you came too early, my
understanding too late. Such fragments were too
small, too frayed, and too inconsequential to be
interpreted, until now. Your childhood remained
cloaked in mystery for many years. So how could I
work anything out for myself?

Let me recount the ways you lived before you were
in charge of me. In those soft times of romance
and useless dreams.
When hope, too sacred to be spoken out loud,
walked hand in hand with you on moonlit nights.
How earnestly you planned your future as if it
was a golden thread.
Never doubting your world vision, never
imagining what really lay ahead.
What foolishness was this?
Where had such thoughts come from?
Shakespeare has a lot to answer for.
Keats, another sinner.
Wickedness all around and *still* you could not see
the wood for the trees.
So, I admire your style but it angers me too.

1920

Most of your early life in those
days was a mystery.
Small fragments are all you gave me.
One: you were the eldest of five children.
Two: your mother died of malaria.
Three: you were twenty-one at the time.
Four: you looked after your youngest brother
after your mother died.
Five: guilt kicked in after the funeral because you
had not helped her enough.

Six: all you used to do was hide away
reading your book.
Seven: that guilt lasted until the end of your life.
Eight: worst of all was your father's adultery
with the servant.
(Your father creeping into her quarters while all
was quiet and the house slept.)
Nine: your incandescent rage hid an unspoken
love for your mother.

1968

Years later when the man you called Father died,
you cried, briefly. But like a tap that had rusted
with neglect, your tears were few. Coming home
from school, hungry, seeing your grief, I stayed
unconvinced, knowing those tears were merely for
the passing of an era. And what might have been.
Like many other things, you never mentioned
this event again.

Still your childhood *was* happy in its earlier
days, until, as adolescence arrived, you overheard
someone calling you ugly.
You were not. But careless words last for a
minimum of two generations.
That inferiority complex you acquired would stay
with you for the duration of your life. As would
your temper, born of injustice.
Both of which you passed on successfully to me.

I am pleased to report that your granddaughter
is very different from us both. And, as an
afterthought, I want you to know, I take the credit
for this difference. Agreed, Heartsease?

No! Smug as always. And wrong, of course.

Evenings in November begin early and with a
feeling of restlessness. Writing all this down is
unsettling, and so I go back to my favourite bar.
Last summer it was different here, bustling, noisy.
We ate our *chiccetti* standing by the counter, or
outside, smacking mosquitoes on our bare arms
while balancing our glasses on the sun-warmed
stones of a nearby bridge.
Last summer a jazz band played in the square next
door to the gondola boatyard.
Last summer it was hot enough to drink the sea.
But on this November night the place is empty
and I find a seat inside. My hands are frozen and
when I take out my notebook, I can hardly hold
my pen. I shall stop.
Turning on my phone instead I read the news.
Although these days the news has got a
whole lot worse. Honestly, there are dictators
everywhere, these days.

Every generation says the same thing. You don't
think we thought this too?
Whatever. I do not wish to argue. I am in no
mood for you this evening.

I have a plate of delicious anchovies and
fried bread in front of me. Better to eat
and not disagree.

Silence.

Where do you go when you vanish?

AUGUST 1963

With love from Mama. A name I crossed out on
the birthday card and refused to utter.
A name I stopped using when we
arrived in England.
A name that somehow shamed me so completely
that I erased it from every single book.
Erasing my former self and, while I was at it, our
shared language too.
Tossing aside the past seemed easier
than I thought.
Then.

Hmm.

Memory works in strange and random ways. Zig-
zagging across my mind in troughs and peaks.
While puzzlingly, I recall with clarity the
butterfly brooch I had so badly wanted. Its
Perspex wings remaining as bright as they were
sixty years before.

Now to my surprise I see there were many things impossible to forget.

Here is a list of what I could not forget.
You, at the butcher's in Brixton, being refused to be served and not understanding why.
You, being dragged along the crossing by two white teenage boys calling you names.
You, wearing your purse around your neck for ever after, because you thought it safer than carrying it in your hand.
Me, in St Cecilia's hall of residence, crying over what had happened.
You, in Petticoat Lane wearing your mustard-coloured coat from 1964. How trendy would that look now.
You, wearing headscarves like the Queen, but unlike the Queen wearing them to keep out the cold.
You, having no interest in British fashion. Mini skirts, maxi skirts, Mary Quant, Biba, the lot.
You, wearing shameful clothes (in my opinion) in order to keep out that insistent cold: thick socks, garish cardigans, terrible orange court shoes.
Your stupid sari.
Me, still buying Vogue in spite of your sneers.
You, saying, are you going out dressed like that?

And some years later when you saw the extent to which He had betrayed you,

You, asking me: 'What shall I do?
Where shall I go?'
Me: No idea. Why ask me? Just leave, isn't that
the easiest thing to do?
Both of us with our mutual package of anger. My
hurt, your hurt.
All of it in the terrible mix.

You thought you had the last word by using death
as a weapon against me. Which is possibly why I
am writing. To have the final say.
I hope you are reading this.
I know your silence is far from the end.

1994

The week after you went, I sat down with a
friend and read your diaries. Only then did I see
with awful shock, how hurt could translate so
seamlessly into bitterness.
Like a trail of blood that congealed so deep
beneath the surface of the skin poisoning
the whole body.
I am dying, you said, thirty years before you did.

So, you named me after a beautiful girl who
lived next door.
Another one of your useless, romantic dreams.
What a pity, you said (spitefully), you could not
turn out to be like her.

I used to wonder what your
impression of beauty was.
Although I wanted not to care, I did.
You have bad taste in beauty, I told you parcelling
up your spite and delivering it back to you.
Return to sender.
It seemed a grown-up thing to do at the time.
No. I haven't, you said, amused by my face.
What a freak you are, I said, getting the last word
in triumphantly.
Why did the Last Word not give me
more satisfaction?

Walking back to my apartment late one afternoon
I see the bridges of Venice have turned golden in
the setting sun. Valhalla's purple shadows finger
the lagoon. Small boats appear dusky in the water
as the fishermen lift their nets in a wide arc full
of glistening fish breathing their last. And in the
distance unmistakable between the yews, is the
island of the dead. Closed now for any kind of
visitors, silent except for the regular ghosts.

Last night my dreams were washed with the
kind of anger we have both come to expect
from each other.
And waking, the old image of you being
dragged across the street by a white supremacist
compounded that dreamlike rage. No passerby
came to your aid, no police officer cared.

Ashamed, what else could I do but erase all
emotions, considering them useless. I had to
live my own life, didn't I? Was not my own need
greater than yours?

Two days must pass before I can recover from
my rage-dream. Two sky-blue days with sailing
boats gathering like flocks of sea birds. Someone
is playing a piano on board a yacht and a sailor
polishes an already gleaming metal sign.
Serenissima.
I smell tar and fish and a late-flowering plant.
Even in November there is life here in Venice.
Today I am just another uninvited visitor who
walks down narrow *calli* without purpose.
Today the city is full of its own mysterious
preoccupations.
O no, I do not belong here.
And I wonder if we belong not to where we are
born but to where we are buried.
Venice can be neither of these two places.

Did you know that the eel swims to its old
home, as do certain birds and butterflies, to give
birth. Before dying.
The eel is capable of travelling huge distances.
What prompts us to think we are any
different from eels?
Remember, the women from Tyree grabbed
handfuls of earth when they were banished to

Newfoundland. All they wanted was to be buried
with soil from their homeland when they died.
Do we spend too much time in the
shadow of our end?
Humans are full of sentimentality.

Today I have been finding it difficult to write to
you. Years of compressed memories are hardened
and pushed down. They have been packed so
tightly into the box marked 'Later', that unpacking
isn't easy. Ripping the layers apart might destroy
everything, I fear. Like that porcelain figure you
loved so much and kept in the glass cabinet in the
sitting room, these thoughts are already fragile.
Why destroy them further?
To write coherently therefore is difficult.

I am thirsty enough to drink the sky.
I am the ghost of the child I once was.
Grief bulges out with no warning.
A country moves through history very slowly and
you and I have already been fighting through time
for many years. No one else has left so deep a
mark on me as you.
A branding with your name encircles my flesh.
But perhaps the way to move forward is
simply to look back?

Solzhenitsyn said that only those who had had
the experience could know the whole truth. He
was talking about the Gulag. Seventy years of

living must surely count for experience. I feel that
at last I can face you as an equal.
I am assuming you know how old I am now.

For some days I toyed with the idea of writing a
memoir but discarded it almost immediately.
Who would be interested in this impression of
our joint lives? I am not famous in any significant
way. The books I once wrote are mostly out of
print now and the articles for the newspapers
have long been forgotten. Even those people who
wanted to do me harm, to kidnap me, and to
prevent me from speaking out, have disappeared
from Paradise. Nothing stays the same. So, what
is there to say?
Better instead to write directly to you. For
only you will be interested. And I need you to
understand what lies behind the made-up picture
I have always presented.

Do you remember what I did after my divorce?

1992

Hurrah, I thought, and I cut my hair in an
attempt to discard that particular past.
You looked surprised when I returned
from the hairdresser. I waited for you to
disapprove, to complain over the money I had
wasted on a haircut.

But you took one look at me and said I looked
young again. Like I used to, you said.
Was that a good thing or not? Naturally I was
suspicious. What was the hidden meaning
in your words?
Afterwards it turned out that the surprise
in your voice was an admission on your part
that I had moved on, finally, grown up and
taken responsibility for my own life. Your
work was done and realising that you were
amazed. We both were.

I had been carrying your sorrow on my
back for years.
It has seeped into my skin.
But now a new skin of starlight spread
across the sky.
Suddenly I remember that rusty old biro you gave
me for my tenth birthday.
And the book with green pages.
And Charles and Mary Lamb's *Tales
from Shakespeare*.

Sunday. There is no sun today.
It is a real November day and I have nothing
much to say to you today.
You want to know what this letter is really about?
When I say that it is all the small things that add
up to a life, do you understand,
that this is what this letter is about.

Animals have no time to examine the past.
They are too busy living in real time to worry
about such things.
We should all be animals.

There is another little matter I have not touched
on yet. But I will come to it shortly.
But first I want to talk to you about
disappointment. Is it possible for disappointment
to be generational? Like trauma.
Because otherwise how to explain our constant,
joint failures.
Has my character been formed, not by Nature but
by observing you. Not by what you said but how I
interpreted your words.
Osmosis gone wrong?

1963

Naturally as soon as we arrived in London the
letters from Paradise started coming. They came
thick and fast. I remember them dropping heavily
through the letterbox: fat blue- and red-edged
airmail envelopes, pages and pages of tiny writing
filling every inch of the paper. Do they even make
such thin paper anymore? Now that we have lost
the ability to write.

1953

You wanted me presumably and so, I was born.
But I think when you saw me you discovered that
all your dead children were locked inside me. At
that point you lost interest. I suppose you were
shocked. Meanwhile I grew up thinking I had
ghosts living inside me. Ghosts who would not go
away and who stared at you constantly through
my eyes. And because of these things I became
confused. You see how you never saw me as I
really was. When I spoke or screamed, when I
made demands on your time, all you could ever
see were those silent, obedient ghost-children.
Who of course demanded nothing but simply
evoked pity. No one should underestimate the
emotional power of ghosts.

Too late I see how different your life was.
Once. And that before I was born and for a
long time afterwards you used to write for the
newspapers. You wrote elegantly and always
in English. Many years later your cousin told
me what I already knew. That your writing was
magical and lyrical and full of understanding of
what good writing could do. He talked about the
power of your words.
You wrote as I wanted to write. Your fingers
on the keys of your typewriter were like the
hands of a painter with her brush. It was as

though you drew pictures with sounds. That's a
compliment by the way.
Possibly the first compliment I've given you, as
praising you wasn't anything I used to do. But
even in those distant days I knew your prose was
so good it needed to be read out loud. It needed
to be spoken so that, when your voice rose and
fell, all the emotions you wished to express were
in it. An actor would have found it easy to read
what you wrote.
Yet you always thought you were not musical.

1963

The night we left Paradise the telephone rang in
the dead of night and the streetlight came on.
We still had many hours to wait before the taxi
would arrive to take us to the port.

As we set sail you were silent. The sound of
the waves seems different when heard from the
middle of the ocean. It is unlike the sound of the
sea from the shore. From the middle of the ocean
the waves are truly frightening.
You looked back and must have thought of the
soil where your children were buried knowing you
would not be buried near them. Isn't that so?
And perhaps also you thought of the
husband who, having gone ahead on a boat

to England was, unknown to you, already
contemplating leaving you.

But having come on that arduous journey,
chasing the monsoons, you lost the art of writing.
Coming to Britain finished off your talent and you
stopped abruptly.
This is the place where the language originated,
where it is spoken, you said, when asked.
I can't compete.
The Queen's English.
There is no Queen's English anymore. Have
you heard how the Queen's grandsons
swallow their words?
Look, we are coming to Dover I laughed.
Those poems had not been written in your
lifetime when you said, I can no longer
write in English.

If you want my honest opinion, I don't think it
was the place that stopped you writing. It was
what had been lost that stopped you.
Too much had been lost, you told me.
At the time I did not understand that this too was
another casualty of our migration.
Once, long ago, your view had been a field full of
rice paddy waiting to be harvested. Only to be
replaced by the streets of London. What a shock
to a pre-internet woman.
Now though, I think, that un-harvested field was
a blessing you bestowed on me, years later.

Perhaps it is a good thing I keep refusing to go
back because that day is etched deep in my mind.
Intact, crystal clear. I *even* remember the music
that was playing on the radio on that last day as
we watched the picture-postcard sunset.
Mozart.

Paradise once lost can never be found again.
Those who inhabited that sacred place
are all gone, now.

You received the news by airmail from your false
friend. Your father was dead.
I hated that false friend and her daughter who
claimed to love you. If I remember
I used to call her the Stick Insect.

The letters continued to arrive. But strangely, for
all the minute details they contained, they could
never leap across the divide.
Hermione, your niece, was thirteen today, read
one of them. We had a small party for her.
Harisha, your nephew, passed his exams and is
now moving to a private school.
Your brother Sugi has got a new job and we all
had lunch together. Everyone laughed a lot.
Oh really, I thought when you read the snippets
out to me. Like I care?
I was thirteen.

I watched as you read their news, eager to be part
of it. What an idiot you are, was my only thought.

Why do you love such useless people who have no
interest in you. Can't you see you are excluded.
And then, you began to send presents.
Oh God, I used to think in disgust, watching you
parcel these things up. Stop being a freak.
A sari bought in that famous sari shop in
Berwick Street.
Cotton dresses with exquisite embroidery
for the new baby.
Whose baby? You weren't ever going to see
it so why bother?
Maths books for one of the children.
Don't they have any in Paradise?
Enid Blyton books that I had discarded.
They were my books, how dare you!
And aftershave for your brothers.
All bought after a trip into Oxford Street on the
number 159 bus.
All wrapped and ribboned.
None *ever* acknowledged. Until at last, you wrote
timidly with the question, 'Have they arrived yet?'
Been very busy, they said, finally.
We've had a festival celebration, they said.
Making alms for the anniversary of
Father's death.
Buddhist monk's event, you know, they said.
And I watched as you accepted these feeble
excuses without a murmur.
But my indifference to these people from a
country I was already forgetting - no I mean

already *forgotten* - grew and flourished. Your hurt,
obvious to me, was on the face of it, of no interest.
Why are you running after them, was all I said.
They don't care about you!
Thus, did I add salt to an already
well-salted wound.

There is no one else I can tell, you lamented.
I shrugged.
That was when you asked me again,
Where can I go?
Asking *me*? I am just a child, I thought.
Then.

The silence that echoed around us was like the
croaking of the bullfrogs in our now distant and
neglected garden.
Even the fountain was waterless, while the sundial
was cracked in three places.
Funny how I remembered *that* little
piece of history.
And like the invisible bullfrogs begging for
water, I ran away.
I had other interests. I was going out to a secret
party that night. Choosing which dress to wear
was more important than your problems.

You used to say you wrote against a backdrop of
the most astonishing hatred. It came from the
most unlikely places.
What the devil did *that* mean?

Random Harvest was your only book. You used
to call it your scrapbook because it held all the
cuttings from your writing. But it was much
more than that and it is my constant regret that
I never rescued it. I believed it would remain in
the house forever. Or if not forever then at least
until I recovered from the shock of your abrupt
departure. If I had it now, I would be better
able to take stock of all those invisible things
you had left me.
But someone got there first. Like a thief in the
night the woman who would replace you came.
Stealthily arriving while I was busy reading the
awful things you had written in your diaries.
What dreadful things we used to say. Successfully
punishing each other as no one else could punish
us. A job kept in the family, I used to think.
And on that very last occasion it was I who said
that most terrible of things. A sentence that
haunts me still.

Although in the end you tried slyly to get the
last word. Your masterpiece, your I-told-you-so
missal, your awful prediction.
Your curses.
Your punishment.
Not that people haven't been predicting dire
things about me for years.
It began with my horoscope which was bound
to be bad. Maybe it should have been called a

Horror Scope? Your diary entries were not half as
bad by comparison.
I can laugh now, sort of. But just to remind you
here is some of what was said.
Get her married off soon or she will be trouble.
She loves meat.
Meat? Where does that fit into the picture?
(Hysterical laughter, Stage Left)
She will be bossy, controlling; just take a
look at the second toes on both her feet.
They are too long.
Too long? How long is too long?
Was I deformed, then?

1953

At this point I was only a few weeks old. Still the
crones of Paradise were examining me.
The word *bad* kept popping up so that sometimes
I was certain it was my middle name.
As someone once said, you will come
to a Sticky End.
And sure enough she came to a Sticky End
possibly because of all the ice cream she
ate, I used to say.

But worse was to come. And *that* prediction was
so terrible that I still cannot say the words out
loud or even write them down.
What possessed that woman to utter them?

I wonder, does a face grow into its thoughts? Is it
unhappiness that ages a woman?
You will not have heard of Botox but I do wonder
if the women use it to hide the unhappiness
in their faces.

Last night I was walking home along the empty
cobbled *calli* of Venice when the friend I was with
suddenly asked me, when was your mother born?
1920, I said, not needing to think. March 18th.
The date was so familiar and therefore of no
importance. Just something I have always known.
But the friend was amazed.
So long ago, he said. Before the war, even?
After one, I said, and before another.
A whole century ago.
Before Botox, certainly.
Mobile phones
Drones
Trips to Mars
Your great-grandchildren
These are just some of the things you have missed.
All those things a long and happy life could
have given you.
Sorry!

And all of this after you had travelled such a
long way. Seven thousand miles. Chasing the
monsoons. For what?
Across seas, leaving, leaving. Leaving sounds like
grieving. Both of which you were well versed in.

1994

The harvest when it came was indeed random.
The only problem being you did not recognise it
for what it really was. Afterwards, on that sad and
final day, someone said,
What a pity. You were the perfect daughter.
Everything comes only afterwards.
Too late.
A tragedy all round.
When I painted the picture that I called
'Waiting for Summer', the man who practiced
Feng Shui cunningly told me it was not a lucky
picture and I should give it to him. So, I did.
Now I have nothing else of you.
Was the whole world against us being close
to one another?
It felt as if almost everyone was in on the act.

When the testing is over God relents, so it is said.
Maybe the testing wasn't quite over?

Yet on the day your eldest grandson was born,
without missing a beat, you made the one
gesture I needed most. How did you know
what was required?
Would you have been a different sort of person if
your mother hadn't died when she did?
A girl needs her mother.
I abandoned you.

Your granddaughter is carrying your
great-grandson. There are a lot of years
between you two.
How does that feel?

Now we are halfway through November. There
is a faint smell of Christmas in the air. I wake up
with a cold. The mosquitoes were biting all night
because of the unseasonably warm weather.
Mosquitoes. We used to be terrified of them given
the history of their deadly bite within our family.

I force myself out of bed and stagger to the
nearby café. A woman glances in through the
window and sees me eating a brioche with my
breakfast coffee.
Marmelatta and café. A wonderful combination
but I doubt you would like it.
Ever since you arrived in this Northern part
of the world milk-tea and silence are your
preferred breakfast.
Conversation became something
you barely needed.

Long before we fled, I remember there was a
time of early morning rising and golden paw-
paws, milk rice, sea breezes, and fried shrimps
salted by the sea.
I remember your laughing.
I remember your lime green sari. The same
lime green that I gave the character in my novel
without even knowing where that colour came

from. It is funny how the imagination transfers
information, gives it new life.

I asked you once why we could not walk on the
best beaches near our house.
That part is for white people you said.
The year was 1958.
The British had taken the best beaches.
But when the British left, the elephants came
out of the jungle.
Wherever the British went they destroyed things,
you tell me now, real bitterness in your voice.
We will never get those days back.

Am I in the middle of a dream or is this a letter
that I am actually writing? To be honest I can no
longer be sure. I hear your voice each morning
when I wake but then when I begin to write you
disappear. Which makes me think I am dreaming
or simply writing into a void. Is there any point
to any of this? After all this time, do either of us
care about the other? There are bridges here. And
water that flows under them.
So, I am more and more uncertain as
the days pass.

I have a confession to make. As you know I have
written many books, novels mostly. I don't think
you have read any of them and for this I am
grateful. My confession is this: I have plundered
your life, your innermost secrets, the things you
buried. I have plundered it without shame or

guilt, greedily, wanting only to feed my books
with your stories.
I have written about the many
deaths you survived.
The longings you held close.
The disappointments you faced.
Most of all the dreams you kept hidden
until the very end.
I knew you would disapprove of what I did but I
couldn't help myself. And I hope you believe me
when I say I did not do any of it for money.
Or fame.
You *must* believe me. Truly I did it out
of pride in you.

Actually, I did it in order to give you
a happy ending.

Here is a backdrop to this letter.
The war in the Middle East rages. Has the Middle
East ever been without war and rage?
Cruella Suella, what destruction do you try to
inflict on others? Your bones are made out of
minerals from the dead stars.
Earth to earth they say but I don't believe this.
Cruella Suella perhaps your bones are different.
Perhaps the soil you came from is not made
of stardust. Perhaps it was some dark star,
beyond the black hole of time that sprinkled
cruelty over you.

Cruella Suella there are those with nothing. Have
you no pity for them?
There are no second chances, here. You
will have none.

Sometimes being offered tenderness feels simply
like proof that you have been ruined.

Another day and still I cannot finish this letter.
Today your voice comes to me muffled and filled
with the sea. Seagulls screamed indignantly and
I take the *sandalo* to the fish market. It is
Friday so the *branzino* is sparklingly fresh
though expensive.
As the man is filleting it for me, I see
the red mullet.
Red, like the red curries you used to cook.
Water curries, you used to call them because the
gravy was just water with a little spice from the
spice mill. Ground chilli powder, turmeric, and
whatever else you had to hand.
I never knew or thought to ask why you called it a
poor man's curry.
But it was delicious.
You, the magician in the kitchen, making
something out of nothing.
A little salt, half a red onion, and a small piece of
fish bought from that fishmonger who exposed
himself as he squatted. I did not have the words to
describe what he did or what I saw.

Red mullet curry. On our last night together this was what we ate.

The last supper.

Tonight, I shall cook my *branzino*. I will cook it with garlic and cold-pressed olive oil. And onions fried to a burnt golden froth. I will cook some broccoli with green peppers, plump as small fingers. My fish will taste of the salt from the lagoon but even so it will not be like the curry you cooked on that last night.

The night of our last supper.

Tonight, I will have a cold glass of white wine to go with my solitary meal.

1993

In those early days of our arrival in this alien place there were no pineapples. Except for those in tins, full of sickly syrup, preserved in neat rings.

We were both shocked, you more than I.

I at least was prepared to give them a try in what was called 'school dinners'.

You laughed. These people don't know how to eat, you said.

There are stone pineapples on the top of Lambeth Bridge, you told me, a few days later. Pity they can't have some real ones in the market.

This sort of talk annoyed me, even then. Why does everything remind you of that place?

Can we not forget it?

After a while I noticed, to my annoyance, that you
lost your interest in cooking. The vegetables in the
market in Brixton were large, swollen, tasteless,
or so you said. I thought you were just being lazy.
Then one day you discovered something called a
peach. Not quite a mango, which we were craving,
but neither quite as tasteless as the apples you
bought. You peeled it, sliced it into segments,
added salt and handed it to me. The salt didn't
quite work. A peach isn't a pineapple, we decided.

Now the nights are drawing in. And although
it is still November there is a kind of bustling
energy to the darkness. A pre-Advent anticipation
that brings with it a longing for Christmas. The
shops are beginning to fill up with *panettoni*
and chocolate mice. There are glass baubles in
the windows and the churches are aglow with
candlelight. There is a star over the *Frari* that
looks as though it is a comet in mid-flight. In
England there is only pointless tinsel. What used
to lie beneath the glitter no longer exists there.
This is the difference between a Christian country
and one that is merely commercial.
You used to get annoyed whenever the
church was mentioned.
Closer to the church, you would mutter sourly,
and further from God.
To a ten-year-old this meant nothing.

But do you agree with me when I say that in
England, with no anticipation of Christmas
in a religious sense, these November days are
dour and formless?
There is no rhythm to the month as the sun moves
to its farthest point.
Surely *even* you, the reluctant Buddhist, can feel
the lack of structure in a country that has thrown
out all belief.
Even you must feel a glimmer of something
magical, here in Venice.

Magic, you say close in my ear, in the same sour
voice I know so well, is for children.

There *was* real magic in Paradise, you used to say
but I only retain fragments of it. I was too small.
The memories I made then were involuntary.
I had no idea how memories worked. Not then.
Although as we stood at the bus stop beside
the railings, I remember thinking: I have
been here before.
Was I having thoughts of reincarnation? At
that young age?

It is when it happens, you snap.
And then you disappear again.
What did I say?

Another morning and my cold has got a lot worse.
My planned trip to Torcello is out. The lagoon
winds will be bitter, driven down from the Alps.

I have been wanting to visit that church for years
but the trip in winter is long and daunting. So
instead, I sit in my apartment drinking coffee
searching for the remnants of your voice.
Tell me, is it forgiveness that I am after?
Did the word reincarnation anger you? Is it
something to do with the ghosts of those children
that were so within your grasp?

It is turning out to be a long day and I dare not
look at what I have written so far. Perhaps it is
formless and of no interest to you. After all you
have heard these stories a million times in one
form or another.
This was meant to be a letter of reconciliation
although I don't see you taking part in the process.
Why is this?
No answer?
Okay, so let me tell you something else. Yesterday
one of my books was rejected. I've had to swallow
my disappointment.

That's easy. I've been doing that all my life.
Oh God, you back again?
We are not in competition, I scream.

I am once again at the railway station café. Two
days have passed since I screamed at you. Look, I
am sorry, but do you realise how impossible you
are? Can you at least wait until I have finished this
letter? I know the days are flying past. If I don't
hurry it will never get written before I return to

England. I doubt I will have the inclination to
write to you when I am back.
Why bother. There is far too much of the past
lying around in my life in England. Too many
things I do not wish to think about.
While here in Venice it is possible to take a 'view,'
to talk a little more freely.
At home, in my house, I will feel an urge to lie to
you, to smudge the facts.
At home fiction will take over.
But writing here is more honest though painful.
And as I sit dreaming of these things, I notice two
Nordic giants, both beautiful, sitting at the next
table. They are another kind of species from me.
Fake gold jewellery adorns every available
part of the woman's body. Thumbs, fingers,
nose, ears, neck.
She is a walking jewellery shop, good looking in a
done-up sort of way.
He is beautiful too though
unencumbered by jewels.
When she opens her mouth, her voice is coarse.
And now, I remember another woman you
thought beautiful. Perfect, you used to say.
Was she?
Your words made such an impression on me.
Why? Were you that stupid?

A teenager always puts herself in the centre of the
picture when it comes to her mother's words. As

I was hoping for a kind of perfection myself, your
words upset me.

All you are doing is dragging up the past.
Spoiling for another fight, Heartsease?

It isn't retribution I want. But I wonder if in the
end this shared past is important only to me. All
I have ever wanted is some kind of involvement
from you. So, please, let's not fight.

Why (I have to ask you this again) did no one help
us understand each other?
There were any number of people who would do
anything to make trouble between us.
He-who-you-loved-so-completely was the
chief troublemaker. He got the ball rolling
and made me hate you. And you, seeing this,
joined in the fray.

Now I know what you were like when you were
young because how you were then was how I
would become eventually.
The neglected child, the dreamy teenager.
Did you sometimes wonder where you got your
personality from?
Had your own mother been that rare
thing, intelligent?

1951

And then, after everything was over and that first
stillbirth was registered came the famous visit
from your Aunt.
That woman.
Carrying curses on her tongue, a cat-o-nine-tails
whip hidden under her sari folds, all six yards of
it. Clip, clop went her sandals as she came up the
hill to visit you, ready to stir the dust of the dead
babies still to be born.
God has punished you, she intoned in a voice that
contained a large amount of thunder.
As you lay comatose on your hospital bed?

After that they were hell-bent on cutting you up
and incidentally severing all connection you might
have had with me. Our private connection floating
off like the string of a kite.
I am mad with rage. Why don't you read what
I have written?

I cannot stop watching the news. Do you
know what is happening in the world just
at this moment?
It was you who taught me, never live outside
politics. Politics, you used to say, is another word
for life. Injustice cannot be ignored. You taught
me all this but then at some point gave up and
instead began reading trashy novels. Romantic
love being your special subject.

Why?
Why did you disappoint me? I thought you were
an intelligent woman.
There are children in camps, I tell you, now.
Children being bombed in their incubators.
Are you listening?
Mothers being killed in front of their children.
Children being killed in front of their mothers.
What a symmetrical story.
And all the while you continue to read
happily-ever-after stories? Haven't you given
all that up yet?

Well, you ask, with one of your bitter laughs, what
can you expect when there are men in charge?

Last night I dreamt I was in Brixton once
again. In the house where we three lived
unhappily together.
I went back to find its rooms changed beyond
all recognition.
The woman who lives there seeming
vaguely familiar.
But, being the person I am, I misread her guilt
for friendliness.

Later when I got to know her slightly better,
I remembered one brief encounter with
her, long ago.
By the front door.
She rang our bell. It was still our bell then.
I answered it.

It was you she wanted.
You spoke to her in a way you never spoke to me.
And then you told her, this is my daughter, you
said. Remember?
She smiled. Large teeth, I thought. A type.
My thoughts wrote themselves on my face and
you said, afterwards
when the door was closed,
You don't like her, do you?
What intuition did you have on that far-off day?
One woman accurately reading a daughter's
expression, I suppose.
I did not know that many years from that
encounter she would steal my inheritance, our
unhappy home, and all its invisible memories.
Your watchful eyes had moved elsewhere, by then.
Unfinished business.

Thirty years would pass before she and I would
meet once again as smiling, she told me she had
no idea who I was. The lie slipped out easily.
Her friend told her to be careful. One day, they
warned I would return and challenge her?
But what use had I for an unhappy house? They
were two a penny.

Who cares?
Memory speaks of things that no longer
matter. Do I lie?
Can one fully recover from an injustice?

In the years that followed shock made me turn
the house in Brixton into a museum. All that
lived there being now vanished. I called it *TRACe*,
hoping art could heal a sorrow.
For it had gone like the *Random
Harvest* you treasured.
Gone like the clothes, the photographs, the small
diaries of hurt, the hidden malice.
Gone leaving only traces of their former selves.
Unable to comprehend, I ran away from it all.
Death needed to swallow up the years before I
could begin to understand.
Time and silence were what I needed most. None
of which was at my disposal. What else could I
do but run away?
While all the time the women waited, patient,
smiling, like carrion, eager to eat off your corpse.
All things come to those who wait, I guess.

Did you know that what I write is always about
the same thing? Always about you. It is as if your
unhappiness is welded onto me, fixed inside like a
steel shelf. Without that shelf maybe there would
be nothing for me to write about? Maybe *this* is
your gift to me?

Another day. Another sunrise. I've lost count.
The sun is shining here in Venice. It throws
small jewels of light on the water. I feel strangely
awkward when I speak Italian. A sort of fake. I
am, after all, just another tourist.

You and I used to laugh together. Not all the time
but when we did you *must* have felt close to me.

1950

I shall call him Jewel-man, for reasons you know
but wish to forget. Jewel-man was shocked when
he first saw you smile. Apparently, the shock was
akin to a bolt of lightning.
I can see him now, in his white tropical suit
standing against the sun on a Grand Central
Station platform.
What a pin-up vision.
His thoughts on seeing you for the first time
were priceless.
My God, he thought. Those teeth!
(Years later it would be he who would have all his
teeth out. One to twenty-four dropping into the
dentist's bowl, counting as they went. False teeth
in a glass each night. Irony lost on you both.)

Don't talk of him in this way, you say sharply.
Have some respect.

1994

There was so much longing in this house, Jewel-
man said after you pushed off.
He could not live in a house of death after that.
Fear sent him out.

Guilt gave him a shove.
Nature taught him the Laws of how he
should have lived.
Karma punished him.
His loss was more than you.
His loss was his memory. That was the worst
of all worlds. What happens when you cannot
recognise your own hand?

But hold on a minute, I am not saying he was a
bad man and the end, when it came for him, was
swift and decisive.
There was, so I was told, a drum roll and then the
police came to tell me.

And now with sudden intensity I remember
something else as though it were yesterday.
It is this: your orange court shoes with
one shoe turned towards the other as you
stepped out of them.
Will I ever be able to forget that image? The
horror of it, the pity?
I wrote to you about that night when you left me,
the night *before* you left,
and the night afterwards.
You would think I would have written
you out of my system by now. Logic would
make one think so.
Yet there is more. How is this so?

1994

A man contacted me out of the blue. He had seen
an announcement in the daily newspaper. Who
put it there? It wasn't me, obviously. I had no
idea that disappearance was what you had been
planning. I thought she loved Paradise, the man
said, puzzled. Why would she have wanted to
leave? The question made me laugh.
No.
Why write to me *after* you left, why not before?
Why write when it was all too raw. My fear of you
was still so enormous, my disbelief terrible.
Perhaps he did not understand fear.
Or what happens when your
mother abandons you.
The lamentation isn't ordinary. It isn't just
someone, I wanted to tell that man.

Well afterwards you saw how I was.
You thought I was so strong, so wayward, so
very difficult.
Another thing amongst the millions of
things you got wrong.

Perhaps those who remain on the shore cannot
help getting everything wrong.
Perhaps that is all there is to this mystery
called 'living.'
Today I am driving myself mad remembering
things that are best forgotten.

Just now I need to stretch my legs, walk, concern
myself with the business of living.
At the fish market this morning I again
bought a red mullet.
And sage.
And *castelfranco*.
I am having fish and salad tonight. Then I shall
write some more. I shall drag up those things that
might be better left untouched.
And sleep the sleep of the disturbed.
Good Night!

By the way, I am constantly accused of an
insatiable desire to bring up the past, things that
are best left unsaid.
Leave the past alone, my father said.
He didn't understand that I live with ghosts.

In England I have started going to a church
modelled on the one in Torcello. And then, in the
late winter afternoons when the light fades, I play
on the grand piano beside the altar. Above in the
blue and gold dome a solitary candle flickers.
Music, like water, holds memory.

Another strange thing is happening in this period
of strangeness.
For years I used to feel a sense of belonging to
this watery city. But today I no longer feel that
closeness. You on the other hand are here with
me. For the moment, at any rate.

People scurry around me while I am
busy thinking.
Without work there is no purpose.
Perhaps you are just a distraction.

1994

For as long as I could remember I had known that
Random Harvest held copies of all your published
writing. Your well-constructed articles that you
cut from the newspapers and pasted down with
boiled rice as your glue.
I remember the book had been specially bound
with dark green tape. Your most precious
possession carried over many seas only to be
thrown away finally.
Like all the rest,
the clothes,
shoes,
photographs,
precious crockery.
All because I did nothing to rescue them?
If you do nothing you are complicit. Isn't that so?
Well, foolishly I am hoping this letter will
return them to life.
Will you be proud of me if I manage to do this
resuscitation?
Will you at last see me as I want to see myself?

Today the news from Gaza is particularly ghastly.
Those in power tell us we should not feel sorry for

the dead. Where you are born matters more than
being born, they say. I sit beside the Grand Canal
indulging in these thoughts.
The laws of the world determine the
wars of the world.
Before you are born you must get so
many things right.
Your skin colour,
Your religion,
Your place of birth.
Do not be born before you sort such things out.
Do not be born if you will need to flee.

We were lucky, though. But although we survived
the blast we forgot our luck.
Forgetting it we looked back at a past that had
grown beautiful in absence.

It *was* wonderful, you say, suddenly waking up.

We left it all behind. How often are those words
spoken amongst those of us who are homeless?
Refugees speaking to refugees.
Off-grid people.
What time is there in the rush to
collect everything?
Why didn't you take what I wanted you to take.
Sixty-two years later and still I am angry.
The water glasses, the books.
The anger has survived the years.
Intact.

1993

Don't you understand, those who flee have no
time to consider such things, you say, again.
You sound weary.
Yes, you add, for the first time admitting your
mistake. I thought what I took was what was
important. And you were just a child. How was
I to know that you would remember the water
glasses after sixty-odd years?
I remember *everything* we left behind, I tell you.
Not just the water glasses.
Banal photographs that take on the stare of icons.
Why did you want *them?*
Because, I say.
My exercise books.
But you got better ones in your new school?
So?
The most important is always left behind.
Oh, shut up!

Another thing that drove me crazy. You did not
want to visit Europe even though it was safer than
the home you left.

Are you going to address all those things that
drove you crazy when you were ten?
What kind of letter is this? And why should I
want to visit Europe? What for?

1958

It is useless. The mango trees are too
large in your mind.
The tropical heat oozes with their scent.
I too remember things. I remember how we used
to walk on the beach at midday. How the heat
forced us to plunge our feet into the clear, green,
unpolluted sea.
Then we'd eat prawns from the beach vendor.

Well then, can you now see *why* that was home.
And Europe isn't.
We had the same experience. But I am more
flexible than you are.
No, we didn't. You were a child.

Always the last word.
Suddenly the anger that is never far flares up.
Can't you see I am trying to write to you, here in
this café. Stop scoring points.
My anger stops me in my tracks.

But there is no stopping you once you get started.
You do not have the kind of fierce love we
immigrants have for home. The word 'home'
is just a word used by people who have only
lived in one place.

Don't shout, Heartsease. We are in the station
café, remember. I am an immigrant *too*.

But you continue with your monologue.

Do you think the people here, these Venetians,
care about what you think? Do you think
if you talk to them about home they will
even understand?
Home means different things to different people.
For us home is not one place. How can these
Italians understand when they do not have the
experience or imagination to enter the dark
spaces we have been in? And even if they travel,
eat exotic food, tell you that your lives matter,
their inbuilt complacency remains. And when
occasionally that complacency seeps out it drives
your suppressed rage.

Speak for yourself, I say, annoyed.
Then I write down your comments in this letter.

1993

Long ago, you told me I would change. I have
a clear picture of you on that day, waving your
hand, taking in the harbour, the sea outside, the
crates being loaded onto the launches.
All this will be a blurred image in your eyes,
was what you said.
But you were wrong.
I *did* smell the ship's engine oil, I heard the flat
sound of the horns. I saw you weeping.

Those patterns woven long ago have never
been undone. They have grown brighter with
each passing year.
The images are sharp and bright and will live
with me forever, impossible to erase. They have
followed me to this watery city. And they enrich
the view wherever I go.
Sometimes even you are wrong.

I think I might have won that round because you
disappear for a few days. Even my dreams are
empty of you. So that when I next sit down at the
café to write I decide to take a different line.

I have three children, I tell you.
Yes, I know. Have you forgotten I knew them?
Yes, but only when they were small. Now
they are grown up.
Don't be silly I know them still. I follow
their progress.
Oh, there is no arguing with you.

You punished me with such cruelty when you said
I was a useless mother, I write, anger flaring.
I had only been a mother for a few days. I fell
asleep. Is that a crime?

Silence.

You punished me for your sorrow, and I punished
you back years later.
I do not say such things to *my* daughter.

Oh, good for you, you say.
I see we might yet descend into another
slanging match.
Well, okay I admit. I perhaps say different things
that she finds cruel.

Silence.

Maybe we don't repeat the same mistakes but
instead find new ones to punish our children with.
One goes on learning the same lessons over and
over again. What do I see in my daughter?
Her stubbornness? Mine?
Soon she will have her baby. Will motherhood
change her as it changed me?

You did not change, you say. Scathingly.
It isn't true.

My cold seems slightly better.
I am halfway through my vacation and confused
as to where this letter is going? Maybe it does me
good to be alone, eating croissants and drinking
coffee, something too sinful to do at home. I shall
go to the tobacconist and buy an envelope and
some stamps, I think. I will finish this letter, or I
will never be able to get on with my life.

But when, with difficulty, I find the tobacconist,
he is puzzled.
I don't sell stamps for that place, he says. Maybe
take a boat and deliver it yourself?

The two men waiting to be served look
strangely at me.
A Venezia vengono sempre dei pazzi.
Mad people come to Venice all the
time, they murmur.
They could be right.

I got my second rejection slip today and am
knocked down by it. Still going somehow. Isn't
that what you used to say?

Rereading what I have written so far, mainly
because I don't want to write something that
might offend you, I feel this is less of a letter and
more of a kind of shopping list of those things
that happened. And I can't help wondering if
that is all that's left of our collective memories?
Just lists. It seems shocking to think the hurt we
inflicted on each other should be reduced to a list.
Your words
My words
How to make a Hate Cake
Method:
First place your ingredients in a blender.
Cooking time.
40 years.
Then bake them until they are burnt. (No amount
of scraping off the burnt bits will make the cake
taste better, by the way. There will always be the
taste of burning present.)
Eat your cake.

And in this way, we can show the forty years of
our life together was just a cake that got burnt.
Would it have been better not to make
that cake at all?

Today as I sit in my usual place in the station café
a gaggle of tourists comes in, their eyes glued to
the menu above the counter. My cold is almost
gone, and I am now beginning to feel a bit more
civilised. Your voice has kept me company on and
off. Today I am going to continue with this letter.
I do not want it to become some sort of useless
diary as I know that will bore you. A documented
life is not what you want. I know because I
read *your* diaries. Those shocking, undissolved
tablets of pure anger. I have carried them around
with me for years.

What is the Venice these tourists see? A Venice of
tramezzini and chocolate gelato.
Next door is a shop with masks of ugly
proportions in the window. I know you would
hate them, obviously. Mask superstition is part
of the culture you were brought up with. So, I
don't blame you.
Masks are for dancing devils, you used to say.
Superstition is all about where you
are born, I reply.
When you splashed me with your superstitions
you did not see that I would be leaving soon to
begin another sort of life in a different place.

And superimposing one kind of life over the one
that I was moving towards, was both impossibly
hard and meaningless. And of course, cruel.

Your fears were the fears of war, of injustice,
of petty anger never defused. They
could never go away.
Except perhaps by passing them on to me.
Handing it down as though you were a runner
with a flaming torch, passing it on to the
next generation.

I used to marvel at how stubbornly held your
beliefs were. I could never have your certainty,
I used to think.
Only now do I see that actually you had very
little of anything.

Your granddaughter is a little this way.
All three of us have talent. Luck, too.
But what we lack are the tools to
harness that luck.
There is a neighbour who lives near me in
England. He swears that education is the answer
for a happy life.
A good school is all you need to give a child, he
tells us, smugly.
He is a happy man, he says. He loves potatoes and
the simple things in life. And because of this he is
a little smug.

So perhaps the answer lies in the understanding
of systems early on, business systems, political
systems, social systems.
How it works in other words. One must wake up
to this early on.

Another question I must ask: If you had been
happy would you have made me happy? Surely
you were happy once. Your school was good, so
what happened?
I must tell the neighbour his theory does not hold
water, at least not in the East.

Home, you once told me, is a word that no policy,
no government, no people can comprehend.
We are wanderers, you said. Yes, *even* you. You
will never get away from that feeling.
I was reluctant to feel this way, but this was
what you told me.

You taught me how to be damaged, I remembered
I once screamed. That's what you taught me.
But perhaps this damage was also your gift to me.

There are scores of people taking photographs
on every bridge.
Mostly they are selfies against backdrops of
famous monuments.
We-were-here written all over their faces.
I envy them their electronic images even if their
pouting mouths are not my style.
Manufactured joy is what we have these days.

See what a wonderful holiday I am having, smile.
Funnily enough the women look happier than
their partners suggesting laughter is more natural
when a man is out with the other lads.

As for you, your smiles were sweet but rare.
Less is more, I hear you say. An excuse perhaps
because there was never much to smile about.
Someone told me that you didn't smile because of
your dreadful teeth.
Buck teeth they called it. They, whose opinion
mattered, at least to you.
And now we are drawing closer to that other
thing we must talk about.
Yes.
No!
Yes. Don't run away, hold still your loyalty
towards him. It no longer matters, remember. He
isn't anywhere near you, now.

1929

No one had either the ability or the inclination
to fix your teeth for you and this makes
me mad as hell.
In that dark place of the deepest 1920s South
what could you expect?
In that village by the jungle, facing the sea, teeth
were not the highest priority.
The nearest town inland seemed a million miles
away with trains running twice a day bound for

the capital city. The milk train at 5 a.m. and then
again at midnight.
Crossing the railway line being safe for the
rest of the time.

No land beyond the cliff face except Antarctica,
you used to say.
What chance was there of fixing a mouthful
of buck teeth?

What could a girl, so bright, so filled with
longing, so like a sponge in search of experience,
do in such a place?
How best to survive?
Intellectual conversation in a village full to the
brim like a reservoir, with superstitious idiots?

Don't call them idiots, you say. I don't like where
this conversation is going.

Maybe not but what chance did an
uncut diamond have?
Nothing was ever going to change for you in that
backwater. No one was going to understand you.
Not a single person.
I am the one to make up for those lost
opportunities.
This is how I plan to make our history
relevant. Trust me.

I trust you like I would trust a python, you say,
rarely-heard laughter in your voice.

I let out a breath.
Even now, after all these years, still, I fear you.
At least you are laughing for the moment.

1929

Your school was in the town of Matara, right? A
big city for someone with such a small horizon
and every morning you stood outside in the
parched front garden with its picket fence, your
uniform, spotless, white, and starched waiting for
the buggy to arrive.
Sleek, blue-black hair brushed and
tied back, neatly.
Your washed face unlined. Those high cheekbones
and eyes as bright as a blackbird's. Curiously
anticipating the day ahead. How could you have
known what the future would hold for you?
What sorrows would come from
reading too much.
Wuthering Heights, Jane Eyre, Shakespeare's
sonnets: God how you devoured them. You were
like a girl who had been denied food.
Girl of the Limberlost. So, did you see
yourself in her?

Whatever neglect you suffered was replaced by
your love for the characters in those stories.
You had pasted a letter in your scrapbook. It was
from a mother to her daughter on the eve of her
wedding. I was a teenager when I came across it.

Sex, marriage, love? Half of me wanted to laugh.
The other half was confused.
Recalling it now with a slight shudder I remember
sneering at your romantic ideas.
Now I simply feel the beginnings of pity.
Was that all you had?

1941

When your mother died, a woman who had
not one single photograph ever taken of her,
everything changed for you.
With her death you were cast adrift. Only your
brothers and your not-terribly-bright sister, were
left. As the eldest it was your duty to look after
the others. You, the cleverest of them all, none as
bright a star as you.
But the unwritten laws of the universe
had to be obeyed.
There was no escape as each night you heard the
creaking of the door and your father's footsteps
going like a rat in the night, to force himself
on the servant.
With his wife dead he needed all the
sex he could find.

At that the devil began his work. Unaware of
what dangers lurked in the capital you stayed
dreaming, untutored, amongst your books.
No one, not even you, could predict
what lay ahead.

A clever, motherless girl, prettier
than she believed.
Your father chasing the smell of other women.
Swatting his children as casually as though
they were flies.

The unwritten law stated that you, the eldest,
needed to be married off first.
The ugly one.
Looking, I now like to think, like
your dead mother.
Who will have her? was on all the
village men's lips.
What a way to describe a girl with skin as flawless
as a bolt of silk and the occasional moonlit smile.
You were doomed.
And eventually, many years later you would try to
see me doomed too.
Feminism wasn't around in 1953.

The devil comes in many disguises.
The Devil Was A Poet.
What a good name for the title of a book.
Handsome, stupid, and generally thought of
as a jewel of a man. Ah! Here it comes! Your
future and my father.
No one said what sort of jewel he had embedded
on his forehead.
A ruby?
A sapphire?

A diamond, perhaps. According to his clutch of
sisters, at any rate.
In those days, love and marriage went together
like a bolting horse tied to a carriage.
Not his fault.
Yes, I know you wish to defend him but let me,
please, just this once, say it as it *really* was. From
where you two now live loyalty is unimportant.
Let's have some historical truth for once.

How well you planned your elopement and with
such great attention to detail.
The day before you left did you visit your old
childhood haunts?
The place where the sea view was spectacular?
The road that led to the coconut grove?
The well where you had drawn water for years?
Your mother's grave?
Did you feel you were leaving your
childhood behind?
Were you excited? Or simply scared?
Had you the faintest idea how your life was
about to change?
Not yet my mother.
Had you been in a daze? Seeing all the old
familiar faces for the very last time?
Did you even eat that night?

More than a hundred years since you were
born, your granddaughter laughs at the
thought of marriage.

She laughs with your laugh.
So old-fashioned, she snorts.
Time, in its wisdom, changes things, albeit slowly.

Now we know that back in the day, how different
things were. And on October 8th in 1950, when
you stepped off the train, into the bright sunlight
of the grand railway station in Colombo you were
heading straight for misery. And the Registry
Office, of course.
Love and marriage. What the hell were
you thinking of?
I know what the devil was thinking.
Through my father's mouth he told me. Although
it did take 20 years for it to come out.

No, I won't stop. You need to read
what I am writing.

1950

A swift glance around the room, checking nothing
had been left behind.
Silencing the dog who whined with a stern look
because *he* knew. You could not risk touching him.
And then your youngest brother, so beautiful,
waiting nervously to escort you to the station.
While the house slept.
A moonlit night with the fronds of the coconut
trees silhouetted against the silvery sky.

A good omen your brother lied, his heart
breaking for you who had been both mother and
father to him. And there was the sound of the
night train as it curved across the coast, hooting
as it came into the station.
And then you were on. Your trunk pushed in by
the brother. Hardly any time for a proper goodbye
as the doors closed and he was swallowed up
into the night.
Only the sound of the waves so faint and far away.

Heat and noise of Colombo. What did
you make of it?
The one brave, terrible thing you were about to do.
For I needed to be born. Yes it was ordained.
The jewels in the Jewel-man's heart sank when he
saw you for the first time.
The famous smile faltered.
Perhaps an eclipse was brewing for was not the
sun a little dim that morning?
What the devil have I done, was *his* only thought.
She is so ugly!
Thus was the first Tinder courtship, that first
Blind Date of the century, occurring. Fifty
years prematurely.

I will follow you to the end of time, you told him.
Fool that you were.
And even though the first night was filled with
cruelty, still, you kept your word.

It was a dry run for that longer life sentence
12 years later.

You are talking rubbish I'm not going to read any
more of this stupid letter.
Maybe not. That is your choice but I am
still writing it.

Silence.
As once more you disappear.

Another day passes and I hope this latest quarrel
is over. In order to distract you I ask again, what
do you make of Venice?
I have a suspicion that you might like all the
tat around. The black and gold gondolas, the
endlessly sparkling glass shops.

As we grew older, I noticed you retreated into
bad taste. Your granddaughter would disagree.
She has a way of turning rubbish into something
more interesting.

After breakfast I decide to take a walk and hardly
thinking I head towards the ghetto. It is unusually
empty of tourists.
In the square are some armed guards. They stand
around in a group smiling. Time has rendered
them jovial. For the moment at least. The sun
shines through the bare branches of a few solitary
trees. Small children run squealing in circles.
Peacetime in Venice.

On the ground are small brass plaques. Easily missable. They are here close by doorways, shop fronts, alleyways. Scattered graves.

Qui Abitava Costanza Misano
Nata 1900
Deportata Auschwitz
Assassinata 5.5.44

Giuditta Aboaf
Nata 1894
Arrestata 5.5.1944
Deportata Auschwitz
Assassinata

Amalia Navarro
Nato 1917
Arrestata 5.5.1944
Deportata Auschwitz
Assassinata

Qui Abitava Gina Nacamulli
Nata 1916
Arrestata 5.12.1944
Deportata Auschwitz
Assassinata

Qui Abitava Lina Navarro
Nata 1926
Arrestata 5.5.1944
Deportata Auschwitz

Qui Abitava Umberto Nacamulli
Nato 1944

Arestato 5.5.1944
Deportato Auschwitz
Assassinato 30.6.1944

Qui Abitava Regina Aboaf
Nato 1888
Arrestata 5.5.1944
Deportata Auschwitz
Assassinata 1944

Qui Abitava Bruno Basso
Nato 1923
Arrestato 18.8.1944
Deportato Auschwitz
Morto 31.1.1945.

Ghosts swim past by like transparent silver fish, fossilised and fragile. I walk across a square empty of all those future writers, the musicians, poets, scientists, doctors, mothers, husbands, fathers. This is a square full of silence and stones. A square where hope was abandoned and Missed Opportunities grew like weeds. A pointless square where both murderers and the murdered have gone.

Those sitting by the waterfront basking in the November sun do not see these silvered ghost-bodies, thin as vapour as they walk by.
Massimo drives his boat full of produce.
Sara's is moored, bobbing on the tide. And all around lie the Melli family.

Amalia Melli
Nato 1894
Arrestata 5.12.1943.
Deportata Auschwitz
Assassinata

Qui Abitava Ada Melli
Nata 1899
Arrestata 5.12 1943
Deportata Auschwitz
Assassinata

Enrichetta Melli
Nata 1890
Arrestata 5.12.43.
Deportata Auschwitz
Assassinata

Abramo Melli
Nato 1902
Arrestato 5.12.1943
Auschwitz
Assassinato

Who will remember them, now?

Nowhere else are the traces of murdered Jews
etched so clearly than here in this first ghetto of
all times. Embedded amongst the stones of Venice
they shine reproachfully at the passersby.
You would have understood this place, I tell you.
A home where there is no space left to hide.
Where behind every door stands fear.

Silence and footsteps. Witness from less than
eighty years ago.
Peacetime in Venice.
Speak memory, if you can.

There is one solitary shop with souvenirs of
these destroyed people. In each possession lies
a life erased.
You will understand, I say again. You who left
so much behind.
You with your life still in pieces.
Your loss intact, still, after all these years.
Shall I buy this silver brooch with its
cloudy moonstone.

The old woman in the shop shouts at me telling
me not to touch the water glass I pick up.
I step outside and the sky is clear, blue, empty
of enemy planes.
Another bomb drops in Gaza.
Another child dies.

It was from you that I learnt how suffering works
its way through the fabric of life. What it does to
a person, how it never leaves no matter how much
soil is used to cover it over.

The party of American tourists walking past
breaks the spell as they drag their overblown
suitcases across the cobbles. The exceptionally tall
buildings in this sad place block out the sun as the
tourists complain there is no network coverage.

Second street on the left, one says.
Be more tolerant, I tell myself.
But the eternal optimism of the American mind,
their positivity, defeats me.
As it defeated you. Once.

Time flies by on sun-tipped wings. November
is on the run.
I need to go back to the story of your old home
and the place where your mother died. The house
with three doors that led to malicious currents
outside. Death when it came did so with stealth,
creeping in through those openings. Letting in the
scent of the sea while malaria settled on water-
filled, empty, coconut shells. Mosquitos with eggs.
A life for a life.
Now I am trying to piece these fragments
together. Your brothers, still small, bewildered.
The youngest boy, your favourite, only a baby.
Your sour-faced aunts admonishing you sternly.
For now, at twenty-one, you must throw away
those books and become a mother to your
motherless brothers. Abandoning all hope.
Bookworm, the eldest boy taunted you, cruelly,
taking his cue from that aunt.
God had begun his punishment. Here comes that
life of hardship he has been promising you.

Eventually though, and with time, a jewel rolled
towards you on what was the empty road of your

life. It gathered no moss but what could be better.
All brides want jewellery, don't they?

Are you mocking me, you ask, as another
argument trembles between us, like
threatening rain.

1950

So, there he was in his velvet jewellery box, a
smile fit to burst, in handwriting so beautiful
that of course, you fell in love. He charmed you
as only he was able while all the time unaware of
the havoc he was causing. Perhaps that was also
part of his charm. He shone like the morning
star. Romance was in the air, dazzling you to the
point of dizziness.
Nothing beats a soft-spoken Tamil man. How
could you resist?
Art, literature (in limited portions, it must
be admitted), the *English* language in all
its glory, rolled up like a chocolate roulade.
In this one man?
Wow!

I've had enough of you and your letter, you say.
This is just utter *rubbish*.

Wait.

You knew nothing of his background except that
he came from a rich, educated family and was his

mother's favourite son. Danger lurked among the
mother's beloved frangipani, hiding in plain sight
and so you missed it.

I didn't miss his mother, you interject. I knew
what she was like from the very beginning.
And it wasn't stupidity but love.

Soon it would be all over.
Jewel-man had many jewels yet so few words,
the gaps between them leaving room for various
interpretations. Let's be honest we both thought
he was deeply meaningful.
He liked to laugh.
Innocent laughter was what he was very good at.
His smile? We've already dealt with that.
But this story is only partly about him.

This evening, towards twilight, in those moments
between sleep and wakefulness I begin to think of
the old house, once again. There were unresolved
emotions in that place, yet we never noticed
how they lurked malevolently. Most things go
unnoticed. Only afterwards does remembrance
return with the scars.
It was the house where you died.
The house where I did most of my growing up.
Like your mother you too died at home. Was this
a gift? From some lesser God taking pity on you?
This evening, I want only to remember it as it
used to be. Not as it is now, tarted up, clean,
scrubbed of all traces of us. The woman who

bought it after your watchful eye had gone, erased
my bedroom to make way for a larger living space.
Eighteen years wiped out with no trace. Thank
your Jewel-man, I thought.
Like the ancient site of Palmyra, or the song of the
wild bird, it was gone for good.
All those years of living, breathing, door
slamming, all those years of looking in the mirror,
opening my wardrobe, studying at my desk.
Gone.

Years later in 1980, looking in that mirror for the
last time as I tried on my wedding veil I thought,
yes, this is the answer. It was a day filled with
hope, rather like your own long-ago hope. History
repeating itself in real time.
But then it too was gone in a flash.
Gone like my adolescence.
Never to return.
There isn't even a stone to mark that life.
Nisi.

2022

The new owner gave me a photograph of the
wallpaper that used to be there. Pink roses, fading
slowly in the sunlight.
Now the new owner gave me coffee. She stared
into my face searching for traces of regret. But
regret was a private matter and I refused to
share it with her.

Disappointed, seeking some reaction, she told me
that a ghost haunted the place.
I think she made it up.
Guilt was scribbled haphazardly across her face
when she saw me at the door for the second time
in her life. I know I look like you and that would
have enhanced the shock.
What lies had Jewel-man told her, about
you, about me?

When the owner saw me she also saw you.

1994

On the day of the funeral, it was your face that
seeped into mine. Sending me a message, were
you, through my own face?
Thanks, I said, but you were kind.
Don't regret, you seemed to say. You have acquired
new knowledge. Come to you by osmosis.
They were the kindest words you had ever
spoken in life.

2022

I hope that house *is* haunted. The house that
should have come to me.
I poured clear water into the cup until it
overflowed while the monk chanted in Sanskrit.
No tears from any of us.

Too late for that, said the Queen of Curses
watching me gleefully.
I glared at her. Don't worry your time will
come, my glare said.
Hysterical laughter somewhere in the
background. Why do funerals do that to people?
Ssh! said Jewel-Man. Don't cry. Think
of the children.
And why do funerals bring out the
worst in people?

On the news today there is an image of a
destroyed building. And then another, this time
a hospital. A picture follows, of a child in Gaza
crying. What price for a child's cry?
Where are those men who did this?
What curse will ever befall them?

1950

As for your father, he never forgave you for
running away with your Tinder lover. Forgiveness
stuck in his throat like a bone on a fish-knife. He
ordered that your name be erased, never to be
mentioned again in his house.
Your father's house had fishbones embedded
all over it. Your father's bones had attached
themselves to the walls of his house. One can only
hope he was happy with his handiwork. After he
died, he left the fishbone to one of his children.

But what did it take for you to return to that
house and the remnants of your family.
It took more than twenty years before you could
admit that your Tinder love hadn't worked.
Eloping is a stylish word. Better than internet
dating even though it amounts to the same thing.
Who else do we know who *eloped?*
Elizabeth Barret Browning, perhaps.
I knew her name as a small child but not for her
damn poetry or her dog. Even then I disliked her.
But then again, had it not been for her I might not
have been born.

Silence.

Are you reading?

Silence.

Have I upset you, Heartsease?

1970

At some point, long after the awful event you
came face to face with your curse-happy aunt who
loved dead babies.
I was with you at her second coming but to me
she was simply an old hag with white hair and
yellowed teeth.
Oh, the curses that come out of primitive mouths
in far-off places.

I remember your brother, the one with his
collection of your father's fishbones, staring at
you in disbelief.

Don't say that.
Why not?
Couldn't he understand that you were never going
to speak to the old curse-witch.

Twenty years have passed, your brother said, *sotto
voce*, do you have to ignore her?
Such rudeness, he shouted, his face dark. The
others in the room were no better.
She never had good manners, I overheard
the servant say.
Puzzled, I looked at your face. Were they talking
about you? And if so, why?
On that day I still had no knowledge of the baby-
curse or I might have killed the woman.

In our time you and I have had our share of
curses, following us around like swarms of
angry hornets.
Do they work?
In the halcyon days of his youth, Jewel-man
laughed at the question. Although when he was
old he changed his mind. Taking no chances,
death being no joke. Having entered the arena on
his eightieth birthday Death had begun to smirk
at him and frightened, he rethought his belief in
the power of curses.

But in those early salad days he lived fearlessly
never noticing that our beautiful tropical island
Paradise was actually swimming in its own
cesspool of hate.
Do you remember how he would kick the
roadside curse-caskets that were left beside
our garden gate?
Rubbish he used to mutter. Utter rubbish!
Christianity being his shield.
You, on the other hand, as a Buddhist, had
no such shield. Plenty of curses disguised as
baskets of fruit followed *you* around. They were
enough for all of us.

If I remember rightly, you told me the evil eye
came in many disguises.
Your father's sister and your aunt were Lead
Cursers, well versed in all its many forms.
Their spells lived on inside you like a wound, a
stigma that bled on a regular basis. Stopping all
feeling, blocking out love, behaving as though love
itself was an overdue eclipse.
You gave them permission to exist. And so,
exist they did.

'Serves Her Right' was an expression used by your
niece, who hated me.
'Serves You Right', was the curse used by the
servant woman who took away my inheritance
after you died.

It was infectious, endemic, back then, in Paradise.

With no vaccination against it you caught the
infection and would have it for life. Sometimes
active, sometimes lying dormant, always there.
So in the end what became of them? Did her
curses save her from dust? Did she take her
bitterness deep into the earth's core?

Perhaps this subject offends you? If so, I am sorry
but my anger will not disperse if I am polite.
So yes, I have always felt misfortune was being
channelled through you.
There, I have said it.
And here is the list of those who cursed me in the
last 70 years:

My aunts.
My uncles.
Your friends' in the poisoned Paradise.
Your friend's children.
My cousins, all but one.
My neighbours.
My father's last lover. Yes, his *last* lover.
My own friends. (Some of them.)
My ex-husband.
His relatives.

That's a start anyway.

So, with the wisdom you now have can you please
stop saying it serves me right?
Can you set me free from that tone of voice?

Don't you know I have always longed
for your blessing.

1993

This is not a confession, but I have an urge
to tell you why I kept the birth of your
granddaughter from you.
It was that single sentence you uttered that did it.
I thought you were cursing me once again and I
was weary of curses.

Later on, I learnt first-hand and to my cost, what
pain such an act causes.
Only experience teaches you this.

1950

But let's get back to your wedding day, shall we?
October 8th in all its stiff 1950s poses, your white
sari, not unlike a funeral sari, embroidered with
your own hands.
Satin stitched.
Delicate
Scattered with flowers that grow only in Europe.
Foxgloves,
Daisies
Bluebells
All those months of work, didn't you know Jewel-
man would never notice?

Did you not know there would be no female
relative to cherish you that day?
Or that I was still many years away?

So, having travelled all night, unable to sleep,
dragging your mother's rosewood trunk (where is
that trunk now?) with your worldly possessions in
it, surely you must have been exhausted?
Did you realise that already you had the
mindset of a refugee?
As for Jewel-man, not yet a father, barely
a husband, well, the circus had almost
arrived in town.
That famous smile, the one that would in later
years drive all sorts of women wild, was strangely
eclipsed on that day.

After the registry office wedding, while all hell
was breaking out within your own family, (your
father having found your I-am-running-away
letter), Jewel-man took you home. And another
sort of hell broke out there. Now, from this
distance, it is comical.
I am sorry but what drama!
A letter left for your father, just as Elizabeth
Browning did. All that was missing was *the dog*!
What were you thinking of?
Sorry. I know what happened next must have
been terrifying.

Picture the scene with my eyes.

The motherless bride. In the photograph, which I
have now lost, your frightened eyes misinterpreted
as severity by the others who saw it.
You unsmiling, Jewel-man's smile was somewhat
in abeyance too, having been replaced by a What-
Have-I-Done kind of despair.
Then the drum roll started, the music began, and
the jewels stopped shining for a short while.

What is the point of all this sarcasm, you ask
me, your voice faint, as though it comes from
a long way off.
Wait, Heartsease. I am retracing our footsteps.
Nothing will heal until I do.
So wait, bear with me.

I don't need a lecture from you. And now your
voice is loud and clear and very angry in my ear.

Do you still not see why *I* wanted a daughter?
Can you not understand even now why your
words pierced my heart?

You should never have a daughter,
was what you said.

Did you not understand the loneliness that comes
from a lack of female company?
No sister, no mother, no aunt.
I had spent years watching other girls walk hand-
in-hand with *their* mothers.

So of course I punished you. It took me a whole
year before I could let you see her, this precious
only daughter of mine. And by then the spell was
broken. You no longer cared.
To be honest it was my sons you always loved.

I don't want your abusive letter. Keep
it to yourself.

It was time to go to your new Anglicised
Tamil family. The moment could not be
delayed any longer.

And there they all were, the brothers, unlike your
own hot-headed ones, silent, handsome, one or
two with an air of suppressed aggression caused
probably by confusion. The sisters in their fine,
silk saris, moving on silent feet. And at the centre
of it, Father and Mother. Your new father-in-law
drunk and jovial.
Okay, you thought, I can handle this, at least.
But she-who-needed-to-be-obeyed was
another story.
The Mother stared at you and said nothing. You
had not heard of autism so you were terrified.
While the gaggle of sisters hated you on sight.
Why?
Ugly, and from the South?
Being Sinhalese. How could these Tamils like
you? And how were you to know that soon the
tables would be turned, and hard-line Sinhalese
would hound these same Tamils and others like

them, out of their homes, burn them, shoot them,
rape them, in a bloody, three-decade-long civil
war, full of a new kind of hatred?
Yes, the tables turned but what use was that to
you who now had joined your roots to his?

On that day, with no idea of how things would
turn out, the whole family remained speechless.
What was this that had strayed into their lives?
You stared back, terrified.

Your mother-in-law, thick-necked and confused
had no idea that soon, too soon she would lose her
favourite son. Or that there were things far worse
than marrying the wrong woman.
How were those sisters to know what lay in wait
for all of them. How their seemingly quiet lives
would be interrupted by politics?
An assassination in the very heart of politics was
the starting gun.
Isn't it always?

Am I going too fast? All this was still
ten years away.
On that night in early October, when the
jacaranda trees were blooming, you listened
to your new mother-in-law speak to her son in
Tamil and although you did not speak Tamil you
understood the tone of voice. One look at her face
gave you the information you needed.

Dinner, and the family dressed up for it.

I know you were aware of how they stared at you
even as they picked up their silver soup spoons.
Aping the British. The thought slipped out
unbidden to be shared with me, years later. The
three sisters made no effort to hide their stares.
When shall we three meet again, you thought,
falling back on Shakespeare.

Finally, the meal was over. The food Anglicised,
and nothing like the hot curries you were used to,
seemed oddly bland. A sharp sense of loneliness
pierced your heart. Home called in spite of your
gold wedding band.
Small sweets next, brought by the servant who
stared curiously at you.
What? A Singhalese girl in this family's midst?
What was the world coming to?
Tamil sweets, Indian food, you think. The
bridegroom awkward and silent too. You did not
know that he was the joker in the family. Then.
How could you when in this ridiculous scene you
were meeting him for the very first time.

Will you please stop this nonsense. Now!
But I am determined to continue, so
please read on.

When the time came to retire for the night you
discovered the small trunk you had brought with
you was still where it had been left by the servant,
out on the veranda.

You had a small present for your mother-in-law
but now, too scared, too ashamed, could not
give it to her.
I have taken your son away from
you, you thought.
At least that was what I *think* you thought.

How the *hell* do you know what I thought?
You weren't there.
Because I am still your daughter.

Night fell like a stone. In the tropics it is always
thus. The geckos came out. From where you came,
in the South, this was an ill omen. They darted in
and out of the cracks in the walls, these ancient
creatures made for curses. A small jasmine
creeper gave off a heady perfume that made you
want to weep because it reminds you of home.
What were your brothers doing, now?
Your father?
Who would tend your mother's grave?
But night had come. It was a night of stars
and anticipation with soft rustlings in
the murunga tree.

She can sleep outside, your mother-in-law said.
No one knew what to do with you.
No one knew this night would be this way.

Enough! It is lunchtime and I have punished you
enough. Like a beaten animal you are now silent.
After lunch I go inside a church partly to escape

the sudden squall of rain and because this letter
disturbs me, too. A group of women are speaking
to the Virgin Mary, heads bowed.
Cruelty used to be a set of rosary beads.
The four women in the house begin their prayers.
Hail Mary full of grace, why has my son married
that ugly girl?
The prayer of every mother in the world.
I should know, have I not prayed away my own
disappointments?
But some disappointments, I tell you, last forever.
In the case of your mother-in-law, healthy
indifference never materialised.
Let us pray, they said.

You saw their shadows bathed, now, in amber
light filtering through the shutters. The servant
woman was making up your nuptial bed.
On the ground, on the veranda.

Your wedding night. Sleeping under the stars
with your new husband, too afraid to speak
above a whisper. Towards dawn did he go back to
his childhood bed?
That tone was set for the rest of your
lives together.
Loveless.
Hopeless.
Pitiless.
Fixed, like the wheel of a bicycle.

Funny, isn't it, how both your families could never
let go of their grudges.

The groom gave you an emerald ring. He had no
money to speak of but he was a generous man.
The ring sparkled in a medicinal way but still you
treasured it. Until it fell off your slender finger
and into the toilet.
Ah well, that was the end of that short-lived story.

Something deep inside me shook, you admit.
This was not good.
It was the first tremor of the
oncoming earthquake.

Yes, Heartsease, you knew, didn't you, the thing
that was obvious to *me* years later.
The lavatory flush was swift.
Of course.
I tried and failed to hook it out.
Did you cry, I ask, unable to stop myself.
Stupid question.

Jewel-man could not afford another
emerald, real or fake.

Will you stop calling him by that name? I
find it insulting.
Okay but didn't he tell you the precious stone had
cost him a whole month's salary?
The payment for a published poem?
Fisherfolk?

Yes.
Was that why you never read that poem again?
The poem and the emerald, it should
have been called.
It would take more than a hundred years before
that thought was aired. By me.

So, on that night of the lost emerald, you both
knew it was an omen, correct?
Green is an unlucky colour, you say.

But it was still a long way from your real and
terrible grief.
And still three years before I would arrive.
Me. One daughter meant to replace two others?
An impossible project, doomed to failure
from the beginning.
Project misunderstood I think.
Added to your basket of failed projects.

I have buried two children, Jewel-man said on a
drunken night, forty years later.

Didn't I tell you not to call him that name.

But the jewel he wore by now was blood red, a
ruby that sparkled dangerously in the light.
My birthstone, he said, forgetting all the others.
A thrown handful of precious stones pierced your
heart. They were all garnets.
Red
Damaged

Dripping blood.
You had nurtured them for years but now no
longer wanted any of them.

1973

The guests, strangers all, listened open-
mouthed to his story.
Forty years ago, he insisted.
Shocked by his indiscretion you felt betrayal crawl
over your face.
Having learnt to fold your grief as tightly as an
origami swan you were naked again with this
sudden confession.

The next day you phoned me to tell me your
story. Maybe in the retelling you thought it
would disperse, like poison gas. But I was busy
doing other things and interrupted, dodged those
fumes, not wanting poison in my lungs. Your
poison, I thought. Then.
And with that thought we both lost out. How
was I to know its significance? I, not yet a
mother, knew nothing.
Now though, I can tell you, as I sit drinking wine
in a bar, *now*, too late, I understand.
Jewel-man had uncovered a secret mound of grief,
soft as a newborn's hair. Leaving it exposed to
the evening air.
A grave exhumed.
Skin pulled apart from a burnt arm.

A wound pushed hard into salt.
A gangrene sore that bled without stopping.
Thoughtless man.
I remain angry with him. Still as a birth.

Your confessions always delivered to me while
sitting on your bed were impossible to bear.
Perhaps some sixth sense told you the bed was
your sacred site, long before you needed one. That
room would be where you were to breathe your
significant last.
Why could I not see, you were not a useless
mother but just a *broken* one?

One learns from the past only when the past has
fled. Burial is not enough.

1950

So that was that.
On that bridal night the unmade baby died
beneath the stars. She was your Veranda baby and
she died with an emerald stone clutched in her
unformed hand. Flushed away as only water can.
A nightbird cried out suddenly making your
bridegroom shudder. What have I done,
was his thought.
It was a thought that would go unanswered
for fifty years. For what was done could
not be undone.

Later Jewel-man's brother would advise him to
run away, leave his mistake behind. But by then
it was an impossibility. The invisible thread, the
golden link that bound him to me, spun tightly,
holding him down until the end. His brother's
suggestion, as tempting as thirty pieces of silver,
was rejected. Let's give him credit for choosing the
hard path to misery. Years later the golden thread
worked itself loose as a splinter might. It moved
through time and slowly he would free himself of
his first mistake only to make another.
No one gave him any advice.

But before all that could happen, we would
leave our Paradise.
His mother would go blind.
And you would commit your first sin.
A woman with two dead children under her belt
cannot be messed with. A sudden surge of power
engulfed you. I gave you that power and you
withheld me from the blind woman.
One foolish deed soon followed another.
You cannot take the child to see your mother, you
pronounced, so adding to your karma.
It was a denial that would return to bite you on
the cheek, the bite being administered by me.
Quietly, slyly, history went about repeating itself.
You are very silent. Is it disapproval I am feeling?

2 0 2 3

This morning, I visited the church of San
Pantalon, again.
There is no rain in the sun-filled sky. I am
thinking of your granddaughter and the baby
she will have in the spring. Foolishly I want her
to make good the great wrongs you and I have
committed against each other.
Sitting in this ancient church I contemplate
her future, my mistakes, hers too. The things I
could never get right when she was growing up.
Are you listening?
Tell me, did I love her enough?
Did I *tell* her how much I love her?
Or how beautiful she looks?
Was I too critical?
Did I drive my tractor over her unformed ego?
And most importantly, will she forgive me?
Suddenly, sitting there in the dark, flame-
flickering candlelight I am afraid.
The old man selling postcards tries to engage
me in a conversation on where I should stand to
get the best view of the ceiling. Can you see the
painting? Can you see it with my eyes?
Do not compare it to the frescos in the temples
you used to visit.

The Catholic Church is not for me, you say
suddenly. Your voice booms as if it comes from
beneath the sea.

What has it ever given me but a
sleep on a veranda?
It is my turn to be silenced.

I know it was your aunt who made you banish
religion. If such a person existed where was God,
you questioned?
Sometimes you would talk to me about
reincarnation. Although you used to add, come
back for more suffering, no thanks.
This letter is meant to change the course of your
suffering. Does it not help? We must not make
enemies of each other, remember.
Jewel-man told me enemies are people who we had
wronged in our past lives.

Now that the month is drawing to a close, I need
to do something other than this letter. I've done
nothing else, not even looked at the book I was
supposed to be writing. So today I have decided
to take the boat to Murano and buy some glass
flowers. It is the sort of place I think you *will* like.
One thing I have come to realise since we began
this communication is your love of flowers. The
most precious of them, perfected in icing sugar,
were kept in a glass cupboard in the living room. I
brought them back after you left but soon tired of
their eternally frozen state of pink and white.
So in a moment of wiping you from my memory
I put them in a box and deposited them in the
loft. Part of you was nearer to the sky I told

myself. There, I thought, satisfied, I will now
forget about you.
Fool that I was.
Years later your granddaughter decided to
resurrect them, four roses and a pink bud. But
they were discoloured and crumbling, pale as the
shadow of their earlier perfection.
Your granddaughter stuck them onto one of her
paintings and there they remain for all eternity.
Your granddaughter has done what
we could not do.
She is a true artist.

I am filled with anxiety over her pregnancy. I
do not want your history to repeat with her. I
have been carrying the burden of your grief, your
loss, your hysteria. Perhaps you truly wanted
things to go well for me but you went about
it the wrong way.

Your granddaughter is a clean slate.
Let her life be unhampered by either of us.

SOMETIME AFTER 1950

After the Veranda Baby died, you moved. The
information on that period in your life is sketchy.
You were reluctant to share it with me.
A mud hut in the jungle?
Is this true?
A small place that you swept clean twice a day.

The lilac flowers you cut from the clearing in the
trees and brought into the house.
You put them in the one beautiful vase you
had brought with you on your journey to
your bridegroom.
Lilacs to bloom in the spring.
Poison gas hiding in the lilac.
Had no one told you they were a bad omen.
No lilacs in the house until there was a death. Did
no one tell you that?

1953

And then I was born and someone, a woman
called Mary, took a photograph of Jewel-man, no
longer a bridegroom but a father now, holding me.
Looking like you. I carry that photograph in my
mind's eye. There we both are, Jewel-man and I,
with the backdrop of the jungle. The photo taken
with a Brownie camera is now floating somewhere
in the North Sea.
I mourn for it still.
And what became of Mary? You scolded her
for not washing her hands before she touched
me. A normal mother's reaction for which
she cursed you.
Ah there it is again. That curse.

This child will grow to hate her mother. Mark my
words. You did not mark them, did you?

Mary, Mary, quite contrary, where are
your pretty maids?
And now, the irony of your granddaughter's name.

Each generation has its own enemies. Why is it
not possible to influence this in any way?
I have forgotten how easily I could like those
people you hated.
Too late, I understand your sense of complete
aloneness when I dismissed your 'enemies',
your mother-in-law,
your sisters-in-law,
your brothers-in-law.
Other people who had been cruel to you.
My enemies were different from yours.
Every time you uttered a harsh word to me, I
turned to them, hoping to be loved.

Yet you must not think I lack empathy, either. It
was there, though faint.

Do you recall how, when I was two, you took me
back to your old home.
The word home confused you. Doing that
journey in reverse had its own indescribable
crosscurrents of emotions. You travelled with the
hopes of yesterday shattered, and the results of
today uncertain.
The year was 1955.
It was hot on the long journey down south. The
train, and then the buggy, consisting of a bullock
cart, took us both to the tip of the island to where

the lighthouse stood facing the sea. Someone,
perhaps your favourite brother, took a picture of
you standing by it, holding my hand. We were
both small against its towering presence.
My hand in yours.
According to your diary you were crying. But I
was there with my two-year-old's heart beating for
you invisibly. The servant opened the gate and let
me in. She took me silently to meet the unknown
grandfather, leaving you standing outside like a
beggar. You did not resist the humiliation. This
was, you understood, your punishment.
The old man sat unsmiling in his high-backed
chair, sarong folded neatly around him. Money
was what he gave me.
I stared up at him.
Years later when I could reflect on this moment,
when my reactions were not simply instinctive,
but more thought out, I wondered what a
grandfather was for.
A few minutes later I was taken back to the gate.
Dirty money, mama, I said handing it to you.
Despite yourself, you laughed.
Why couldn't we stop the clock in that moment
and acknowledge our loyalty for each other?
It lay folded in my hand, the dirty money,
one hundred rupees of it, a testament of my
feelings for you.
And then we began the long journey back
to the capital.

There were still thirty-eight years to be
lived together.

Even on the day he died your father was unable
to utter your name. He took stubbornness to a
new level, handing it down to his son and onwards
through the generations.

After that trip to Donrah, you became silent.
What was there to say now all the bridges
had been burnt?

Now the aunts, your sisters-in-law, visited us.
For it was my birthday. A token visit with a
token birthday present. Maybe they thought, as
their favourite brother would soon be leaving for
England, a tea set for his only daughter would
be a good idea.
And I for my part loved those cheap tin toys with
their garish dark design that would soon rub off.
The aunts told me the tea set was expensive and I
believed them until it rusted and broke.
By now civil unrest was on the rise and thoughts
of leaving the country, aired by Jewel-man,
filled you with terror. You who had gone no
further than your village. Going abroad seemed
further than the moon.

1957

The Lady Card Reader told him that life was
about to change. She could not say if the change
would be for the better.
The child, the woman said, would go her own way.
Funnily enough she could not predict the
second great loss that was on its way. Perhaps it
was a good thing.
You were still writing your pieces for the
newspaper. It was the only skill you possessed
and for once and for the only time, the world
took notice. It was a golden moment that
would never return.
I too was living in a dreamworld of my
own. Occasionally being beaten by you for
my naughtiness.
This *was* the 1950s. What could one expect?
Sparing the rod had not become a mantra, yet.
But there were baby sparrows nesting in the
rafters of the cavernous barn.
Then the servant broke a clay jug full of water,
spilling it onto the parched earth. It seeped across
the ground like blood.
Bad luck, you said. There will be a death.

There was no death. Not then at any rate so
we moved house again and I was punished for
destroying a present from you both. In reality it
was the beginnings of my lifelong obsession with

all-things-collage but neither of us realised what
was driving *this* interest.
This child likes to destroy things, you told the
neighbours who shook their heads at what you
had given birth to.

Don't exaggerate, you say.

But it was true.
The punishments went on and on as did your
editorial work. It kept the roof over our heads.
What Jewel-man did was a mystery.

I told you not to call him that, you say.

The roof leaked and you put a plastic sheet over
the bed. When the monsoon came the plastic
sheet (white squares with red roses) leaked too.
Hastily you got the buckets out. The rains were
torrential. I loved the sound of it falling on the
corrugated tin roof above me. I still like sleeping
to the sound of rain.
It was a blissful childhood despite the
scolding from you.
Crows invaded the little garden breaking the Peter
Rabbit plate you bought me at great cost.
All that money to be destroyed by a crow? In the
end the tea set disappointed me too although I
said nothing, not wishing to hurt my father. Soon
I placed the cups, the saucers, and the teapot
back in their box and stopped playing with them.

What was the point of playing with a teapot that didn't pour?

One day, around this time, Jewel-man took me to the Ideal Home Exhibition. Ours was not an Ideal Home by any stretch of the imagination but you had your dreams so, on the way back from a rare visit to his childhood home, we stopped over. It was unbearably hot, and you did not go with us. Perhaps you were up against a deadline for an article for the newspaper? Or maybe it was because of the planned trip to see my paternal grandparents that stopped you. I remember very little of that trip.

Two other things stand out from that day.

One was of my aunt, the oldest of the three. I had been allowed to look through her pile of *Woman and Home* magazines sent to her from England. On one page there were paper cut-out dolls, made for children. Again and again, throughout the visit, I kept going back silently to that page. Then I asked Jewel-man to ask her if I could tear it out. She refused even though he begged on my behalf. Never mind, he said on the way out, understanding how disappointed I was. She is a peculiar woman.

The second thing that I still remember was at the Ideal Home Exhibition. There, amongst the 1950s drawing rooms and kitchens built for the British ex-pats, I was given a free donut. Dubiously, I accepted. I had never tasted

anything so wonderful. After two bites I saved
the rest for you, carrying it home on a train that
sped across the coast. I still see the suppressed
delight on your face.
Why then did we both forget that moment?

I was five when bad luck came to the sister with
the magazines. It announced itself in a series of
phone calls made to a neighbour in the middle of
the night. Jewel-man left hurriedly as dawn was
breaking. The sky was pink with warning and
the crows had begun their noisy cawing. As he
stepped out of the front door a lizard fell on Jewel-
man's shoulder.
An ancient cold-blooded creature believed to
predict the future. I remember you shuddered.
Bad luck wasn't simply confined to you.
Was it bad luck?
Although I had no idea what was happening,
Jewel-man's hasty departure, the falling lizard,
and your face terrified me.
Half-explanations and misunderstandings
were nothing new.

'Don't go', I cried a few days later as you dropped
me off at school.
I won't, you lied.
There was talk about the jungle. The *jungle*?
I knew already that the jungle was everywhere,
waiting to employ its poisonous snakes. Death
lurked amongst the thick covering of trees,

death with his sword. You were my only anchor.
Jewel-man was in some emotional state I did not
understand. So, I screamed and screamed.
Don't go.
I had no idea what a funeral was. Uncle Edwin,
dead? What did that mean?
I screamed and screamed. What if you too
had a funeral?
Don't go, I shouted.

It turned out the lizard *could* predict the
future, after all. Uncle Edwin, the aunt's
husband, had died.
Years later I learnt they had been driving through
the jungle and he had closed his eyes for a second.
The Coca-Cola lorry had been in front. What was
it doing in a jungle? No one said, no one filled in
that bit of information.
Ever.
Uncle Edwin took the brunt of the crash, dying
instantly. Thereafter that aunt would carry the
evidence across her face, playing violin music on
the gramophone, never touching the piano again,
and hating you for remaining alive.
Jewel-man identified the body at the mortuary
and broke the news to the aunt. The smashed
car had been stripped of every single thing from
leather seats to steering wheel and tyres. For
some reason this was what seemed to me to
impress everyone.

Villagers in the jungle.

Her bitterness towards us both would remain with her scar. A pity really because her gift of music would pass seamlessly on to me.

There are five days left in November. The Christmas tree has gone up in St Mark's Square. It sits between Theodore and the crocodile and the flying lion of Venice. It is said we should not walk between the two pillars on which they stand. So much superstition would, I am sure, make you feel at home here. The shouts of anger, the loud laughter, the sudden spurts of emotion, all these things should surely feel like home.
I stare at the Christmas tree.
It is large, like my first Christmas tree but with none of the scent of the forest that I remember.

That first tree was brought home by Jewel-man's cousin balanced on his bicycle, stolen from a nearby forest.
He was called Anton and was possibly the only relative of Jewel-man who bore no grudge. He came late on Christmas Eve while I slept. And you both worked through the night making decorations. When I woke at dawn it was the scent of forest fir that filled the house.
A smell I have never forgotten and seldom have encountered since.

Forever after, in this cold Northern hemisphere
where we ended up, Christmas is tinged with
sadness for this loss.

That morning when I woke I saw the paper stars
made by you from wrapping paper saved for
months. And most wonderful of all, a paper doll,
bought at huge expense. My heart's desire.
A triumph over the newly-widowed aunt. Was
there a gleam in your eye?
You, the Buddhist embracing Christian
customs just for me.

In all the dreary Christmas days that followed,
year after year in cold, grey London, no fairy
lights or baubles would ever hold such magic.

Mass in the cathedral by the sea followed.
The scent of the ocean mixed with incense, the
wooden crib, rough-hewn and shabby.
Christmas 1963 was very different from
Christmas 1955.
Other things were lost, too.
And you no longer had an appetite for any sort of
Christmas celebration.
We began to separate from each other, love so
present on that day in 1955 was becoming a dirty
word hidden under the debris from the brutal
uprooting. Slowly indifference developed.

On your very last Christmas with me in 1993 in
a different city, older now, you sat bewildered

watching your grandchildren, excited as a swarm
of bees, run riot.
You must have wondered how you had come to
this. How had your life evolved in this alien way?
What had you done to cause this chaos, what
thread had you pulled that now would never go
back into its spool?
Nine months later you would be dead.

Christmas is coming to Venice.
It is here in the sudden drop in temperature and
the small glass Christmas trees that are in every
glass shop. I want to buy one but do not. It is a
kind of superstition that stops me. It is all about
fear. There is new life in my family soon and I am
frightened of disturbing the luck. Luck, I know,
is fragile. So, I do nothing. I do not prepare for
this Christmas.
Fear, I think, is one of the ways you
exist in my life.

A woman in the café where I am sitting helps
an older woman, her mother I suspect going
by the physical appearance, to put her hat on
before going out into the bitter wind. Seeing the
look on both their faces, the weary affection,
the familiarity of a lifetime, I feel a sharp
stab of loneliness.

I am heading towards the end of a life cycle.

Like the birds who cross continents to hatch their
eggs before dying, I too have done what I have
been put on this earth to do.
Now I have to face the inevitable.
Old age is so sad. But, I tell myself, the
tapestry woven by a younger hand will survive
even if I do not.
Small comfort, I suppose.

Today I am finally going to Torcello. I am writing
on the boat and all along the horizon line the
Alps are etched sharply. Blue with the cold. I am
obsessed with the Alps in the way Jewel-man was
obsessed with apple trees. Every time we passed
an orchard he would fall into raptures.
Do you remember? You used to be driven mad by
this obsession.
None of us understood why those trees were fixed
in his imagination.
As the Alps are in me, now.

When the children were born, Jewel-man planted
one tree for each of them in my garden.
But when we moved the new owners refused to let
us take our trees with us.
So now those trees continue to grow on some
distant plot of land.
Somehow the thought pleases me.

The sun is shining as the boat ploughs its way to
Torcello. The air is clear and cold. How wonderful
it would be to see the distant Alps every day.

Overhead a plane, its wings tipped by the sun,
flies over the lagoon. As I too will fly very soon.

When I left England, it had been dark. The coach
driver taking me to the airport seemed weary,
the tungsten light over Oxford lit the desolate
rubbish-strewn city.
Huge land-gulls feasted on rotting food spilling
from plastic bags.
Finally I boarded the plane and that was when
I thought suddenly of you. How you hated
flying. As I do now.
You see how I carry you everywhere I go.
But then we arrived, and I was shocked all over
again at the burst of light that greeted me.

And now an empty Torcello. Only half a
dozen people live permanently on this, the first
island of Venice.

Winter has settled in, the trees are bare, the little
gardens have been tidied up leaving only small
traces of summers past.
A few children's toys lie on the damp
ground, a tattered flag of the Lion of Venice
flutters in the wind.
Hard to imagine that a thousand years ago there
were refugees fleeing pestilence and war, escaping
to this untamed backwater.

There have always been refugees, you say,
quietly. Always.

Inside the basilica is rose stone and gold, marble
dust and faded frescos.
Mosaics burnished brightly as if only
recently embedded.
I am reminded of the temples you took
me to as a child.
The gilt and chanting.
Religion, I know, has let you down. You tried
rationality although that didn't work either.
Staring at the mosaics I see some of your distrust
has rubbed off on me.

Buddhism is not a religion, you correct me now.
But a philosophy.
What should I believe in, then?
Only in women, perhaps.
Hail Mary Full of Grace.

Well, the Basilica of Santa Maria Assunta is a
pagan place, Heartsease.
That's all right, then, you say satisfied.

The prayers of the ancients can only be accessed
through imagination. No human intervention can
unlock their secrets, for imagination is the sole
portal to other worlds.
I wish I could stay a little longer here, but the cold
and the wind are harsh. I pass a small makeshift
café with an open fire on my way to the boat stop.

People are drinking wine and eating fish from the
lagoon as they huddle around it. Long ago when
I was last here the pomegranate trees were full
of fruit. Now they have been pruned and stand
guarding the weathered stone statues of goddesses
in the garden of the priest-house.
The trip back to mainland Venice is icy. The
sun has sunk into the water, the sky is troubled,
and the horizon line of mountains has vanished.
There is a disabled man on the boat. He is
handsome but childlike.

You see, you say, there are others
worse off than you.

Did you know that my first novel ended with a
boat trip passing the little islands that nestle in
the waters of the lagoon, past Torcello. I wrote it
nineteen years ago.
Your hand was in the writing of it.
I wonder if you were autistic and masking it?
Did you know? I am surrounded by autism. I feel
alone amongst people who think differently.
I am, I think, just five years away from your
age when you died. Loneliness is something we
have to live with.

When I woke this Sunday morning it was from a
dream of a fisherman, bent double in order to pull
in his catch. I had taken a photograph from the
boat but looking at it again it carries none of the
magic of the actual moment.

And then in sudden surprise, I remember those
water glasses we had.
Venetian glass etched with the figure of a
fisherman bringing in his fish.
The glasses I wanted us to bring on the boat. You
said they would break so we left them behind,
giving them away to people who could not
reach their history.
We never found others like them again although
every time I go back to Venice I look. They
remained in my mind like a chimera, magical and
alive in my imagination. Until I saw the image of
the fisherman and realised it wasn't Venetian glass
I was looking for but an image.
Like the Perspex butterfly brooch you could not
afford to buy me?
Let me remind you. You had picked me up from
school and were on the way to the railway station
when I saw a woman selling toys. I cried so much
that you must have felt sorry for me and so the
next day you said you would buy it. But when
we went back it was no longer there. Perhaps it
never had been, perhaps it was simply part of that
wretched imagination of mine.

In the news far-right power is marching across
Europe. Fear has entered the arena after so many
years of peace. I am afraid for my children and my
children's children.
Luckily this is no longer a problem for you.

Was the day you died the best day of your life,
I ask? You gave up the ghost on that day, giving
the problems to me. I must not start to think
in this way as the old anger flares up, unbidden.
Why did you leave me so ill-equipped to deal
with my own life?
Silence.
I remind myself this letter must not be
about my anger.

Another baby is killed in Gaza even as I write.
Must I not mention this? Can art and literature
ignore politics? This letter isn't just about us.
It started in rage. Now the rage has turned a
corner. Do you feel that too? Are we getting
somewhere at last?
You are lucky that you don't have any news where
you are. Only water to float in.
Why do they say earth to earth when we come
from water and return there?

Bend like the trees in the monsoon, your brother
Sugi told me in a rare moment of empathy. So I
did but I broke anyway.
Penniless, without you, I was cast adrift. For
poverty, like potholes, is the new order of the day.
This generation understands.
Make money, work in the City, have as many
expensive holidays as you can, burn out, get
exhausted, and then lie on a beach and read
a beach novel.

Is this why my novels are no longer of any use?

Here are a few more things you need to know
about these last twenty years that might have
escaped your notice.
We had a pandemic.
A lockdown when no one was allowed out. Think
of it as a curfew that went on for months.
We formed what were called bubbles and
lost the ability to communicate with those
not in our bubble.
We have not recovered from this siege mentality
and so our health problems have grown.
From this a few of us have come to realise that
humans need other humans.
Not everyone understands this.

What happened after you left was as bad as what
has been happening to us since the pandemic.
First, your sister lost the man she was to marry
because of the shame you brought on your family
by eloping. And not just eloping but going *over to
the other side*!
Then the neighbours shunned your father whose
pride was such a burden to him.
It was no laughing matter at the time.
Each generation lives within its own primitive
system of stupidity.
So you were trapped as I am now.

Your granddaughter is twenty-seven weeks
into her pregnancy and my fear is growing
with her baby.
I know too much, maybe that's where the
problem lies with us. Or maybe my imagination
is overdeveloped. I notice your granddaughter
has a similar stubbornness to you. She marches
through life, scattering her mistakes left right and
centre, fearlessly, oblivious to those around her.

Women only need other women to confirm and
reassure themselves. If they do not get this they
seek a man to give it to them. The irony is no
man can because no man understands fully a
woman's needs.
The word we have for this disjunction these
days is 'autism'. But I think it is something
else altogether.
Who invented the word autism? Was it a woman?

I had another memory of a conversation
with Jewel-man.
Once long ago he told me you were the temple girl
he abused in some other past life.
It must be true because the Lady Card
Reader told him so.
Inevitably after that he never set foot in a temple
again for fear of the Gods attacking him.
Did the cards not show him that if he continued
to abuse you emotionally in this life you might
return again to harm him?

Something I want to ask you.
When, on that early morning, as he came into the
ward to see you, unaware as yet that your Veranda
Child was dead, what were your first words?
Drugged with morphine, alone, beyond tears,
what were those words?
Will you share them?
Can you see why I am so afraid for
your granddaughter.
Is it true that only experience can make a
person understand.

Today I bought presents for the unborn baby.
Then I hid them in my suitcase, for I am now
superstitious, and don't want to tempt fate.

1963

I remember the dresses you embroidered for
your baby. The one that never came. Even today
I hate your choice of colours. And now at last I
understand why you chose blue.
The baby was a girl. Those clothes were your
longing, alone. Secrets, too precious to be spoken
out loud. Of every mother the world over.
So now I hide these presents from myself.
We took your first grandchild, a boy, out for
a walk amongst the concrete tower blocks of
Stockwell and that was when you told me how
much you had wanted a son. And when the baby
died, guilt at this innocent desire kicked in.

I wanted a boy, you said.
Stupid, I thought, not seeing it as a cry
for forgiveness.
Thus, was communication lost in the
wind yet again.
Conversations wrapped around mistaken words.

Stop, you tell me. Your voice is like ripped cloth.

The past is tucked into little pockets of what
is our present.
The past never goes away.
The past: recycled.

Your loneliness wrapped like a python around my
new-mother bewilderment.
Your mind, like baby yarn, knotted up, impossible
to disentangle for the next forty years.
Did you not know what you were doing to me?

In the end the dead babies were too much for both
of us. The burden was too great.
No one came to help you and by the time we
were walking around the concrete blocks it
was all too late.
The dead babies were hell-bent on creating havoc.
Was it a coincidence that one of them
was called Rachel?
Neither man nor woman, Rachel, who hates
music, has returned as a neighbour, punishing me
for the sins of others.

1969

Years later, in spite of your grief, hating the long
flight, still you went back, Heartsease.
Why?
Perhaps you hoped to reconnect with those you
had left behind, then finding only the indifference
of the years that had passed you were silenced.
They too had done with their anger and their
bitterness and had moved on.
So you, after years of living in another kind of life,
found the past had changed colour.
The brothers had married.
Good marriages, they told you.
Your sister eventually found a man who could
cope with the shame of your marriage.
A man too stupid to know what shame was.
There were nieces and nephews who told you
they loved you.
Did you really believe them?
Jealous of the use of that word I turned my face
away from you.
The distance between us was growing
insurmountably.

They sent you back with presents: jewels,
precious stones.
Amethysts
Black sapphires
Aquamarines
Moonstones

A few scatterings of diamond chips
Gold.
There was no frankincense nor myrrh though.
You see, you told me triumphantly.
What did you want me to see?
How they love you, still, you said.
I saw nothing.
And wanted none of them and in any case, I had
lost that strange language I once spoke.
So communication was impossible.
There is a photograph, one of three remaining,
where you stand by your favourite uncle,
unsmiling as always. He was a man, a lone relative
who had gentleness in his face. Who had had the
ability to comfort you.
One lone man who did not give up on you.
One lone relative and you standing amongst the
cacti, framed by tropical heat.
Your mother-in-law was meanwhile going blind.
For her there was absolutely nothing to see.

Your brothers watched you nervously for now
you were a different species, one they had
no experience of.
Only now, with the distance of time was the truth
revealing itself.
Time was uncovering what had been
hidden for so long.
The brothers stared at you, shocked,
uncomprehendingly, their suitable wives
silently by their side.

Since you had left the island English had been
lost. A series of wanton nationalist governments
had seen to that. No one could understand your
polished speech.
How strange the wives must have
thought you were.
How unlike their manly husbands.
And in order to show this difference they hid
their unease by being deferential towards you.
Which you correctly interpreted as indifference.
Did you not know there would never be warmth
between you no matter how much you tried?
And however far you searched you
would not find any.
For the love that was present, hiding amongst
adolescence, was in England unseen by both of us.

You therefore concluded sadly that what these
wives with their obedient children had, was love.
Their husbands, your brothers appeared to
be turning out better than Jewel-man. How
had this happened?
And so you brought your sadness to England with
you on the flight back away from the sun.
It was heavier than the luggage in my head.

I am back on the waterbus a few days later,
people-watching.
Nothing much else to do.
I am stuck in my own head.
What's wrong with me?

The girl is young, the boy handsome.
As the boat sails under the Rialto bridge, I think
too handsome for his own good.
Another Jewel-man.

Later in a bar, another couple stares in opposite
directions, boredom written on their faces.
I sit and wait, reduced to people-watching.
This letter is very unnerving. Should I be writing
it at all, stirring up the dust in this way?
Lunch arrives beautifully presented.
Worth the wait.

1970

The poison was everywhere. Science could
not change the mysterious ways in which
Paradise worked.
And so, a terrible misfortune befell your brother.
Cupid the culprit yet again.
Two cousins marrying, a recipe for disaster that
came with no warning.
One more lovechild lost
Yet even as you offered comfort from across
the seas, there was no acknowledgment
of your own loss.

Jewel-man did not know the child but, instead,
polishing his gems, wrote a poem to mark her
death. He had forgotten his own loss by now.

Like a sphinx, as usual you said very little.

Tomorrow there will be only nine days left
in Venice. New life stirs at home, and I am
eager to get back.
The weather remains bitterly cold, and it
has grown dark as the year turns. Maybe
there will be snow.
Rereading what I have written I see I am
uncovering a lifetime of decay. An ancient
archaeological dig that interests no one except me.
And, I hope, you.
We have had interesting lives is what I now see.
When I return, I will put these events in the
museum called *TRACe* for others to see.
I will put them on a shelf with museum labels
marked 'universal' and 'memory'.

Look now, see, what noble dignity is in these
things: a Bronze Age bowl, blackened and
beautiful. Lift it gently from the cabinet for you
to hold in your cupped hand. Only one hand is
required as it is so small.
Peer inside and you will see human ashes. And
nestling at the bottom is a woman's bangle.
Made for a slender arm.
Flesh and gold melded together. Burnt together
though eternity.
Only gold remains.

Moving through this museum of
memory, look again.

Here is a child's dress.
Torn, stained around the neckline.
Whoever hand-embroidered the dress has long
gone and no amount of heat steaming by the
specialist restorer can remove the stain of blood.
Fifth century Coptic. Found in a grave.
A mother's grief tumbles through the ages as fresh
as the moment of burial.
A child preserved by cloth.
A grief understood by every woman.

When does fiction become fact?

This morning, I am writing to you on scraps
of paper as I have lost the earlier letter. This
morning the watery city feels like a prison, so I
write fast. Time here is running out. I feel some
urgency to reach you.

There are three doors I need to unlock before I
can get into my apartment.
The outer door from the street is no problem.
Then the flight of beautiful stone steps and after
that another door slightly harder to unlock. This
has a bolt with a metal rod that is suitable for a
prison cell. Only then will I open the door into
my apartment. This too has a bolt with another
vertical lock.
Locking in memory, locking out
secrets. Which is it?
In a city where there is hardly any crime why are
Venetians so fascinated with locks?

This secretive city has locked in its memories from
prying eyes for centuries.

With nothing else to do and with this self-
imposed exile and this letter almost at an end, I
decide to visit the *Accademia* gallery.
I don't believe you have ever set foot in a western
art gallery. Why did you have so little curiosity
about the great collections of western art,
even in London?
The Constables
The Titians
The Turners
Even Gainsborough's rich satin cloth could
not interest you.

The answer lies, possibly, in the lids of the
imported biscuit tins with their royal crest,
you say. On the lids were cheap reproductions
of Constable's *Haywain*, Turner's sunsets,
Gainsborough's *Girl on a Swing*.
We both saw them all before you told me they
were part of a colonial culture you hated.
That royal crest on those tins made you shudder.
Your views are still too ingrained to be shifted by
a visit to these galleries.
But on this occasion, and for the purpose of this
letter I do not pester you to come with me.
Maybe I even understand you a little better.

Lunch is at Zucca. A pumpkin flan with ricotta,
pumpkin seeds, and slivers of carrots.

I wish you were sharing my lunch.

You called your second angel child Rachel.
And now she has come back to haunt me.
She draws tombstones on her window without
knowing why she does it.
Someone is driving her from beneath the
earth's surface.
The local vicar said the devil hates music.

Jewel-man's passion was to leave the island as fast
as he could in search of a better life. I remember
him staring out to sea crying.
I have to leave, he said and leave we did. After that
his ambition vanished, evaporated into thin air.
Going back was never the same for him. What
was lost could never be recovered. But that day
as he stared out to sea, he was crying. The sea
looked grey. Only on the horizon between sea
and sky was a thin line of gold. Was this the gold
we were pursuing?

Two gondolas glide by. You and my father would
have taken a trip on one of them. Jewel-man was
keen on being a tourist and you would have simply
followed him. Except of course he would never
have taken you with him on a trip abroad. And I
was spared the embarrassment of watching you
step into one holding your sari up high, faking
a smile as the boat wobbled, reminding you of
that other boat.

From the distance their silhouette looks magical against the setting sun and I think for the first time it was this image that was etched on the water glasses we left behind. Here is the boatman crossing the lagoon, his oar dipping in and out of the water. So, this is where my obsession with Venice has grown from. I thought it was the water glasses but now I see it was the gondoliers.

Old fake leather seats
Garish colours, red and yellow
The Venetian flag of a rusty lion
Fake plastic flowers
Kitsch, your granddaughter's favourite aesthetic.

There is autism in our family, you say suddenly.
What, I ask? What brought that up?

And then you say, as a refugee the thing you want most of all is to stay in one place. In peace.
Is this why you showed no curiosity? For
Britain or Europe?

It is the 29th of November already. Today I realise how bored I am with this city. Walking the same streets, eating the endless *focaccia*, drinking another glass of wine, what am I really doing here? And then I realise I am no longer stopping to look at one perfect view after another. I walk staring at my feet avoiding the dog shit on the ground, frowning at the tourists who block my path. I no longer struggle to speak Italian. It

seems pointless. Something is happening, some
alchemy is at work connected with this letter. It
would appear that, as if by magic, I have conjured
you up completely and therefore my usual desire
for company has waned. You are suddenly back:
a better you, a companion to a better me.

Is this what happens when we stop being tourists?

Only your granddaughter fills the gap.
Fear passes over me again as I
anticipate this new life.

Do you know I have not touched the book I am
supposed to be writing?
Did you know the name your granddaughter
plans to call the baby? Can you guess? Yes, that's
right, she will call him after the man you ran
away to marry.
I wonder how you will react to your great-
grandchild. Is the distance too great for there to
be any real connection.
He will be born one hundred and four years
after you both.
You see how the past joins so perfectly
with the future.
But what can you tell him these hundred
odd years later?

I want you here. Now. Participating
in the present.

And can you make me a better grandmother than
I was a daughter?

1987

Do you remember when Jewel-man suffered his
first heart attack?
You withheld the information from me for
three whole days, during which time he
might have died?
Power at last, I thought.
Power over his sisters, and over me.
Shocked, I hurled insults at you when I
eventually found out.
Righteous anger brought no satisfaction
to either of us.
And just when you could have him all to yourself.
Your foolish little power struggle was really yet
another cry for help.
He loved me more than you, you know, don't you?
So little love was left over for you.

The last day in November. Once again I am on my
way to Murano in the rain. High water. When it
rains in Venice it comes as a monsoon.
Your granddaughter is in the hospital having a
test and I stare at the water anxiously.
The waterbus is crowded and very low in the
lagoon. We are enveloped in a soft mist. The
umbrella palms dotted on the island look out of

place in all this wetness. I am going in search of a
chandelier because the one at home is broken.
My mobile phone rings on the way back. Your
granddaughter has gestation diabetes. A South
Asian problem, she is told. I feel pangs of guilt
in my chest. And all those things I have written
about are beginning to haunt me all over again.
I am not a nice person. Maybe I should stop
writing altogether?
I want to go home.
We are the same family of women. Why did I
not take a photograph of the three of us together?
Another oversight on my part.

Five years since the cheating started, when I was
seventeen and in the middle of my A-Level exams,
eight years after your third child Rachel was gone,
you sat outside my bedroom door howling like a
wounded animal. Irritated, I tied a rope across my
door and left through the huge sash window in
our Victorian flat. Off I went to meet a forbidden
boyfriend. What larks, I thought.

Sometimes when having truanted school in order
to see this boyfriend, I would find you sitting in
your bedroom with the cat on your lap.
The room where you would eventually die.
Ignoring you I went straight to the kitchen in
search of food.
Love being a hungry business.

Not having much strength, you had made only
a little food.
Never enough, I thought, raging.

One day you told me that the cat was
your dead baby.
She's nuts, I told my friends laughing away my
confusion. Whole hazelnuts!
Meanwhile, unknown to you, my own life was
the mess that came from loving a man thirty
years my elder.
Nothing beats a mother's anxiety.
You were too strict when I was growing up, your
granddaughter says, in an accusing kind of voice.
Just you wait, I think.

On the way to Murano we pass the island of the
dead in the heavy rain. Superstitiously I turn my
face away and take no photograph.
All around the *Fondamente Nove* are the echoes
of my children's summer footsteps. How many
summers did we spend here.
I feel lost.
I am drinking too much, living in my thoughts,
dining with ghosts. Is this wise? Self-indulgent?
Somewhere there is the sound of a Beethoven
piano concerto, but I struggle to identify it,
momentarily losing you in the process.

DECEMBER 1ST, 2023

Finally we have arrived. Although it is still in the future my new grandson will be born in three months' time on March the first .

Now you began to fight. The great love that is Jewel-man, the recipient of your crazed adoration, began to dissolve into fury. Those fights, long overdue, were terrible. You were discovering that the jewels were embedded in claws of clay. Often when he was drunk, he was overcome by a desire to sleep. Anywhere really, the bed (you threw coconut shells on him while I, aged three, watched), and on the last occasion on the bathroom floor hugging the toilet.

Why do I write of this?
Who on earth can be interested in this hopeless story? I have waited a hundred and twenty-four years for the balance to be redressed. Now, time has done its work, stripping out all emotion, except perhaps laughter.

1957

One of the coconut shells you threw at him fell near my feet and I picked it up, curiously examining it. And then having examined it carefully, threw it at my father.

I wore a white dress.
A white organza dress.
I was five.

When I was eleven, I wrote down all the things
I wanted most in the world. None of which
I actually got.
I wrote it in my stamp album brought by your
Great Love for me. I had no interest in stamps.
Or books on the solar system.
I just liked writing lists of things.
But how could I find the words to tell you this?

Years later when I could have anything I wanted
(within reason) I wanted nothing.

This is what I have discovered as I sit writing
in the watery city. Given long enough, nothing
except memory matters.

Take that away and you are lost, I tell you.
Impressive, you say, sarcastic as ever.
But I insist, it is my own discovery.
You are silent. Does this mean you agree?

Do you remember the first essay assignment of
my O-Level English?
We had been studying George Eliot. *Mill on the
Floss*. Remember?
Ah you said when I carefully recounted the lesson
with the teacher who was racist.

Ah you said, you are being taught properly,
learning English in the country where the
language originated. How wonderful! You were
thrilled. All the things you could not have you
were giving to me.
What satisfaction that was. All your sacrifices,
your terrible trip across the ocean, travelling
the monsoon winds on a bathtub of a
ship, and now this.
So then why did you force me to choose science
subjects at school? Why want me to become a
medical doctor?

Racism ran like thread through our lives,
destroying everything we touched.

You and I had one holiday together during which
you were silent. Perhaps you were scared of
my unpredictable temper? Although I believe I
behaved myself.

The sun rises on another day.
This letter is the first and probably the last time I
will talk to you.
I have been coming to Venice for almost thirty
years and I see now I have begun to think like you.
However lovely this city is there is something
else I have been searching for. I have searched
all over here, down every narrow street, on every
graceful bridge, on every stone lit by the setting
sun, but have until now not found what I have
been looking for.

Until now.

In the end I have only my memory but is it
a false memory?
And now there is one last thing I remember.
One last thing that caused me a sharp pain
that I could hardly bear. I *have* to know if you
remember it too.

1963

After you lost the baby, you insisted on visiting
the woman who had also been pregnant at the
same time as you. I do not remember her name:
Maggie? Maya? Miria? No idea.
Her baby had been born safely. So why
visit, I asked.
You can play with her daughter, you said.
Do you remember?
What madness was in that decision?
So, we went by bus to her house.
A rich woman. You were taking the clothes you
had made for your baby and I, even at the age
of nine, knew it wasn't too good an idea. So I
dragged my heels, pulling at your arm, whining.
We took two buses that took forever as we stood
waiting in the blistering heat. Finally, we arrived.
A high wall with bougainvillea cascading over it
and the scent of frangipani in bloom.
The electric gate opened, and we went in.

Inside the woman and her two daughters stood
unsmiling. In her arms was her newborn son.
You were not allowed to touch him so instead
you handed your beautifully wrapped gift of
dead baby clothes, and the servant took them
and the baby away.
Then the woman and you sat and had tea together
and I was instructed to go away with the woman's
daughter. Reluctant to leave you alone with
this proud woman, I saw you wanted to be rid
of me so I went.
We don't want your dead sister's clothes, the other
child said. We have a little brother not a girl. And
your clothes will bring bad luck.
So, we had brought our bad luck along
with us, I saw.
Soon after we left. I did not know it but you had
recounted for the first time the full horror of your
daughter's death, for the first of many repeated
times. Why, I thought. Why did we go?
Was it your empty arms that had propelled you?
Were you punishing yourself?

That child born in a rich woman's private
maternity ward would be a man of sixty now. His
sister, if still alive, would be older than I am.
And I want to ask you if all their
pride was worth it?
What was this love you wanted?

Two weeks later we set sail for England.

Why has that memory of that terrible afternoon
surfaced so clearly here in this beautiful city?
Who were those people and how did you know
them? Can you please tell me? Was that woman
part of the photograph taken at the studio
when you were all girls? Four of you. But the
photograph is now lost. You were the most
beautiful, high cheekbones, long straight hair,
talented. Why the hell didn't you smile?
That look remained even on the day you died.
The others all made suitable marriages to
men from their own town, Sinhalese men,
rich, pompous, ugly. Why did you fly so
close to the sun?
What had you wanted? Poetry?
The handsome one had wanted only pretty
women. Pretty, in his terms, meant white.
Your skin was like silk. How do I know? Because
I have your skin, don't you know?
We made the slow journey back in silence,
changing buses, dodging the beggars and the filth
on the road. Until at last we were back in our
small house with its vista of the ocean. Soon we
would be on it.

Yesterday I visited the first church of Venice.
San Giacomo. In disrepair. A statue of the
Virgin Mary and a list of names praying to her
in Lourdes. Then a small notice saying it was the
chapel of the dead.
I fled.

The crumbling church and its atmosphere
were so powerful that I even erased the
photos from my phone.
It is cold now as I throw open the doors of the
past and try to let the demons out.

When the testing is over, they say, God relents.
Maybe the testing isn't quite over in that case?
Not until you agree with all I have written.

Remember how I painted you afterwards? I
painted you against a winter landscape looking
towards a distant horizon.
Waiting for summer, I called it. For a summer
that never came.
We were just ships that passed in the night.
Tell me, what is the likelihood we will meet again?
All I have of it is a small photograph.

How could I know your life would be snuffed
out so abruptly.

Today there is no sun. Only endless rain on *calli*
that are filthy. Another sleepless night scrolling
through my phone. You won't know what
I mean by that!
Or maybe you are sneakily keeping an eye on
what is going on in the world.
Maybe, and here I hesitate, you are
watching over me?
No. Too good to be true.

Although I have heard the dead never really
disappear but keep watch. Certainly, the day of
your funeral I looked in the mirror and saw your
face had transformed into mine.
I hope I am not writing simply to myself.

Is seventy the moment when you think of old age?

What were you thinking on that very last
night? I know you mentioned my name.
Words of absolution.

I don't blame her after all, you said.

And why did my father not tell me until a year
had passed? These important words?
What little importance he put on your power.
Afterwards he would not sleep in the house.
There is too much unhappiness there, he told me.
Too much longing.
That was what he said. More or less his last
meaningful words to me.

Here then is news that might have escaped you.
Things are no better in your absence. Do you
know about this thing called global warming? The
unpredictability of the weather. The scorching
heat in summer, the constant storms in winter,
and hardly any spring.
The green lung of the earth, the Amazon forest, is
slowly vanishing.
And Asians now have all the power.

Now Brixton is a fashionable place.
And everyone wants an Irish
passport after Brexit?
Beauty has a new meaning.

In the station café where I sit with my
usual breakfast of coffee and croissants the
public address system announces the trains
as they come in.
Napoli
Roma Termini
Milano Centrale
And then over the border -
Parigi
Lyon
Zurich

How easy it is to slip over the border should
you wish to do so.

Can I love a place where I spent only ten short
years? Is it you I love and not the place?

Walking across St. Mark's Square at night I ask
myself, what foolishness made me ever think I
could call this place home?

A beggar stands on the bridge near Frari, cap in
hand, homeless no doubt.
I am homeless amongst the homeless. The only
difference is I have a plane ticket in my pocket.

My last day in Venice. My bags are packed ready
for the flight back. Mostly they are full of presents
for the unborn child.

I am ready to leave. The dream has gone but
something else, something more enduring
perhaps, has replaced it. When I return home, I
will reread this letter. Will it make any sense at
all? Or will it present itself as just the ramblings of
a lonely woman?

Why do we write? The answer evades me. Some
months ago, I stumbled across the book *I Will
Never See The World Again*. Stuck in his tiny cell
in prison, with little daylight, the writer used
scraps of paper in order to write. Maybe we write
in order simply to remember? Would you agree?

Now there is one last thing I must do today and
that is to visit the public park across the canal
from the ghetto. It is called Parco Savorgnan, a
place I visited ten years ago.
On the other side of the canal are the remains
of the famous wooden doors. But the park when
I get there is no longer as I remember it. It has
always had a melancholy air but now it is derelict.
It begins to rain, and the drunks sit huddled over
their cigarettes. The shutters in the apartments
are closed or broken. There is rubble everywhere
and the old well where they hid the Jewish
children has been closed up. Only through one
window can I see something of the glory of the

past. A solitary chandelier hangs high above
in the ceiling.
One rose bush remains. It has not been pruned
for years, I suspect. An air of silent menace hangs
over the place.
Not a single child's voice can be heard, no mother
calling out anxiously.
But beyond the *vaporetto* stop, past the wide
opening of the lagoon, beyond Mestre and its
industrial port is a clear blue view of the Alps.

I am going home.
Grey, hopeless, cold.
I leave at four in the morning.
I am the only person in the waterbus.
All the lights on the Grand Canal shine on the
water. The casino is shut. Along the way the
statues are lit up.
Everywhere is silent. There are cascades of fairy
lights in preparation for Christmas.
The city is ready for the festive season.
Mist in the air. Everything ghostly.

I know that Blighty will be dark and wet.

I see your face as it was at the end.
Was it the face of peace?

What was lost cannot be replaced, you say.
Finally. I hear the sadness in your voice.
It is enough of an admission.

ACKNOWLEDGEMENTS

Thank you to Jennifer Grigg for believing in the book. Thank you to Jane Glennie for designing the cover, typesetting, and your understanding of the text. With thanks to Daljit Nagra for the inspiration for the line on page 37.

And thank you also to J.B. Bullen.

For all those refugees fleeing war who made new homes elsewhere.

ISBN 978-1-910804-28-5

1st edition. First published 2025
by Green Bottle Press
83 Grove Avenue, London N10 2AL

© Green Bottle Press

Text © Roma Tearne
Cover image © Jane Glennie

Design by Jane Glennie. Typeset in Jenson family.

Printed and bound in Great Britain by Clays Ltd, Bungay, Suffolk.